—MAP—
— of the —
—SALINAS VALLEY—
—BEET * DISTRICT * Nº 3 —
— of the —
— SPRECKELS SUGAR COMPANY. —

Scale : 40 chs = 1 inch.

JULY 1905.

SPRECKELS SUGAR COMPANY
July '05, Spreckels, Cal. Sheet Nº 193. A.

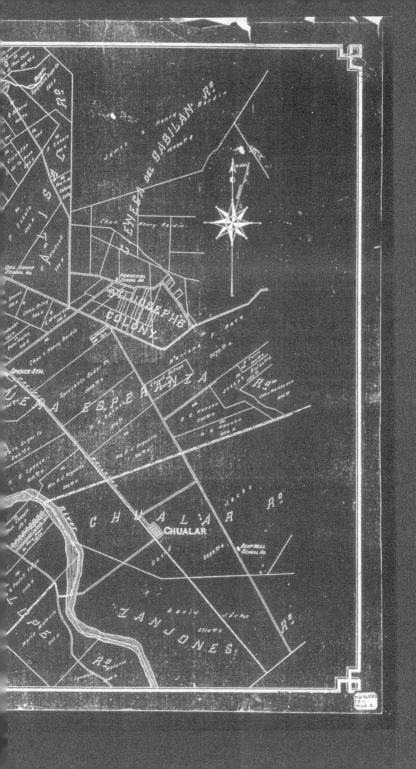

CHILDREN of the WILD

KRYSTA TAWLKS

Monster Ivy Publishing

To the men in my life:
Husband, Pops, Kyle, and Lil Brudder. Thank you for your
deep-rooted hearts.

Chapter One

The pinch in my chest is bothering me again. It's been burning for a few days now. Feels like hot embers crackling under my ribs. Like there's a fire lizard trapped in my chest, spitting flames. It's flaring up on this dry, quiet morning, like an old injury. It doesn't hurt, though. Just comes at a bad time.

Like right now. I'm stuck pacing my room in my long johns. A ratty pair of pants and a thin cotton shirt hang off the foot of my bed, ready for a day in the fields, but I can't go outside. Not when I feel like I could burst into flames.

I slow my breathing and take in the quiet corners of my room. I think about cold things like blocks of ice shipped in from the Sierras, the needling spray of the Pacific Ocean, and the Arkansas winters of my childhood. Meanwhile, my insides boil hot as a wood-burning stove.

This isn't working.

I take a turn around the room and pass by my window. From across the lawn, I catch bits of chatter. Looks like my brothers and sisters have started the day without me. They'll be knee-deep in their chores before I manage to button my shirt.

I'm feeling annoyed, and I kick my hamper as I pass by, knocking a pile of dusty clothes to the floor. That's when I hear something—a soft scratching sound. It's coming from the back corner.

Suddenly, I forget all about the fire in my chest.

"That you, Finn?" I duck to the floor, searching for my youngest brother. Did he sneak in when I wasn't looking?

A raspy hiss croaks near my ankle, and a scaly creature thumps along the floorboards toward the door.

Definitely *not* Finn.

I creep up to a reptile with yellow-orange scales and blue ridges above its eyes—a fire lizard.

Of course.

"Hello, friend." I grab a blanket and prepare to trap him.

At first, the critter shrinks back and flops against the door. Then he pauses, squints at me, and an orange glint lights his eyes.

What's he thinking?

That's when the door bangs open, and a tubby little face with a dusty mop of hair peers into the room.

"Finn!" I say.

"Morning, Elbert," he says, his syrupy eyes sparkling. He grins and scoops up the lizard. "Ha! Got him."

I jump forward. "C'mon. Hand him over. He could be dangerous."

As if to prove me right, the lizard cocks his head and belches. Beads of fiery spittle shower the rug at my feet. Finn stomps on the rug with the heel of his boot, same as he would a puddle—with a hop and a giggle.

"Okay, okay. Now you really do have to hand him over." I reach for the lizard, but Finn steps back and eyes the hallway.

He wouldn't dare...

He turns and stumbles down the hall, heading for the kitchen. I'm still in my long johns, so I throw my pants over my shoulder, tuck my shirt under my armpit, and chase my stubborn little brother.

I enter the kitchen where I spot Vida kneading sourdough and feeding the wood-burning stove. Before I can pass, she steps in front and blocks me with an arm as thin as a broomstick, but hardened with years of scouring cast-iron pans. Her steely gray eyes dig into mine. "Elbert, where are your pants?"

Pieces of her chestnut hair lay flat against her sweaty face as she moves stiffly in her cotton dress. Must be hot out. I wouldn't know. Everything feels cold these days, especially compared to the heat burning inside me.

I glance at the back door, open just a crack. Finn must have slipped out that way. "Gotta go," I say and push forward.

Vida holds her grip. "Not without your pants."

I sigh and wiggle into my clothes. While I'm busy with that, she shoves a handful of blackberries under my nose. "Also, try these."

A pop of flavor fills my mouth. "Go get Finn," I say between bites. "He's got a fire lizard."

Vida shrugs. "He'll be fine. Are they too sour?"

More panic, mixed with that strange, crackling heat, churns my insides. "That lizard spit on the rug. With fire."

"Must be the heat," she says, without a hint of concern. She points to the berries in my mouth. "Judging by your face, I'd say they're too sour."

She's right, but this is not what's important right now.

"At least tell Mom and Pops if you won't help," I say.

She glances down the hall and frowns, her face darkening. "They're not doing good right now, Elby."

So, Mom and Pops are in their room again. Must be having a hard day. I'm sure it doesn't help we've reached the month of June, the worst of all months. Not for everyone, just

3

for us—the Dowden family. But no one will talk about why it's so hard.

Not that I have time to chat. Finn needs me *now*.

With my pants hiked to my waist and my half-buttoned shirt hanging off my shoulders, I shoot my older sister a glare and hop through the back door before she can fuss about something else.

Ahead, Finn is scurrying across the yellowing lawn like he's just robbed a bank. He heads for the rows of sugar beets and straight for Peto who stoops in the distance.

I cup my hands around my mouth. "Peto! He's got a lizard!"

Peto glances over at Finn and grabs the bucket next to his leg. He plops the bucket in front, and Finn throws the lizard into the pail. With a sly grin, he says, "See? I got him."

I grab his shoulder, harder than I should. "Don't ever do that again," I say. Prickling heat creeps to my face. "That lizard could have really hurt you."

Finn yanks back. "Ouch, Elby! Peto, tell him to stop."

"Stop," Peto says without lifting his head from his work.

Tears form in little Finn's eyes, and I know I've taken things too far. I kneel and wait for him to calm down. "I'm sorry about that, Finn. I was just worried, that's all."

He nods. "It's okay, Elby. I know you get scared sometimes."

His words surprise me. Scared? When do I get scared? Before I can think of anything to say, Finn twists out of reach and runs toward the orchard.

Peto pushes the brim of his hat above his eyes. "He's right, by the way. You were kinda scared for just one fire lizard."

I shake my head. "I wasn't scared."

"You don't have to keep protecting him so much. It's been years now since... well, you know."

4

Yes, I know. Finn almost died once, a few years back. But as far as I'm concerned, that's a good reason to protect him.

I heave a sigh. Or maybe I'm overreacting.

I join my older brother in the dirt as he brushes his wide hands alongside the leafy rows of sugar beets, searching for smaller weeds. He looks like a grown man the way he hunkers down, but he's only sixteen.

I guess some might call that grown.

He pauses and yanks on something—another fire lizard. He's got it by the tail and tosses it in the bucket. I peer inside and see at least four lizards scrambling around. Yup. Fire lizard season is here. If we're not careful, they'll start burning things down.

If I'm not careful, I'll start burning things down.

Another wave of heat hits me, and I bend over like I'm about to hurl.

"You okay, Elby?" Peto says with his rumbly voice.

I should tell him. Now is as good a time as any. But...

There. A shiver—much different from the twisting heat—rises in my gut like a warning. It crawls up the back of my neck, followed by an overwhelming urge to keep my mouth shut. My stomach tightens like I'm about to betray myself. Like some part of me knows a secret the rest of me doesn't.

"Elbert?" Peto says, a little louder than before.

I open my mouth, ready to speak, but a new wave of nausea spills over me, followed by that deep-down urge to keep quiet. I swallow, forcing it down.

Maybe I *am* going to hurl.

"I'm pretty sure... there's something wrong with me," I say.

Peto grunts. "Yup. Definitely something wrong with you."

It's a fair joke. I'll give him that.

"I'm serious," I say. "Did you ever have this pinch in your chest? Kind of like a candle got lit inside? But it doesn't hurt?"

He tilts his head. "Yup."

My mouth hangs open. "Well? What happened?"

"I've always had something pinching my chest. But it hasn't acted up since I was about fourteen."

Fourteen? I'm fourteen. "So, it goes away?"

Peto rubs the peach fuzz on his chin. "I'd say so."

His words give me hope. Maybe, if I'm patient, this heat will go away on its own.

"Talk to Pops if you're not sure." He pauses, then adds, "You know. When he's around."

Yes, I know. All too well.

I lean back and glance at the blond hills lounging in the distance, not yet touched by the morning glow. The sun is working its way up the horizon, warming the valley floor. A patchwork of sugar beet crops and grazing fields stretches from farm to farm, stopping short of the Upside Down River. Back near the house, I spot a horse-cart packed with hay, probably our neighbors to the right. The cart wobbles up the lane, heading for the dirt highway, and melts into the road beyond.

I squint for a bit, trying to pick out the wagon again, until something skitters across my ankle. I twist around to yet another fire lizard. This one's extra chubby.

I kick my leg, but the critter hangs on.

"Peto," I hiss. "Can you grab him?"

The lizard slides off and hops onto my other leg. His beady blue eyes fix on me, then flash orange. "Hurry up. Before he spits."

But Peto has stopped moving. "Uh... Elbert. Are you seeing this?"

I glance back. Fire lizards, at least ten of them, maybe more, are wiggling their way to the topsoil. They're squirming —toward me. I hop back a few steps out of spitting range.

Peto tosses a lizard with his toe. Another one spits blue flames at a sugar beet sprout. He stamps the spittle with the flat side of his trowel. "Have you ever seen them chase you like that?"

I pry off the lizard clinging to my leg and send him flying. "No. This is new."

Peto grabs a rake and starts scraping three at a time. "We're going to need something to dump these in," he says.

I grab more buckets and a pair of rakes from the storage barn, and we spend a good part of an hour clearing the field of the fire lizards. It isn't easy. As soon as we finish one area, more lizards jump to the surface and squirm toward me. It's terrifying, the way dozens of these fire-breathing critters slither to the top of the soil, cock their squinty eyes, and scurry over. For every lizard we scoop up and dump into a pail, five more appear, hissing and scratching their way past the seedbeds, always toward me.

"What do they think you're made of, fire ants?" Peto mutters as he swipes a family of lizards with his rake.

I race to the house, fill two buckets of water, and return to the swarm of lizards. I swing the pails wide, splashing the scaly backs of the creatures. They hiss and scatter for the wild grasses. And just like that, not a lizard is in sight.

Peto and I sit in the dirt with our backs to the sun, panting. I'm trying to make sense of everything that's just happened. Fire lizards chasing after me? Could this have anything to do with the heat growing in my chest? Deep down, I know I should be worried, but what am I supposed to do? Avoid working the fields?

Peto wipes the dust off his trousers and tips his hat above his eyes. "That was weird, Elbert."

I agree. Very weird.

He strolls back to the house while I pause to take another breath. Seconds later, the fire in my chest slows to a whisper.

Finally.

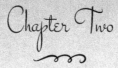

Chapter Two

Only a few days have passed since the lizards swarmed the fields, and already, more strange things are happening. I woke up to burn spots on my bedsheets this morning, and now my room smells like smoke. Lately, my skin turns red every time a breeze passes by, and water makes me nervous to the point I skipped bath day last week.

I'm sure it's just a phase. I *hope* it's just a phase. Just like I'm hoping Finn's sleepwalking is just a temporary nuisance. He's been sleepwalking again, more than usual, and since I'm the lightest sleeper of the family, I'm the one going out to grab him. Usually, I catch him before he reaches the fields. Convincing him to go back to sleep is another story.

But today, I feel like something bad is on its way. Maybe it's the quietness around the house, or the fact Mom and Pops are keeping to themselves again. Mom is in her room, and Pops took Fuzzy Lips on a ride out to the hills.

Or maybe it's because today is the worst day of June. But even on the worst days, the farm needs all the help she can get.

I'm supposed to work with the young ones in the orchard, so I go outside and find Trinna pushing an empty wheelbarrow through the dirt. She pauses, her eyes latch onto me, and she drops the wheelbarrow as if it were a pile of trash.

"Elbert! You're here." She leaps into a run, her gangly arms swinging, ratty braid swishing like a horse tail. She yanks me to the first row of peach trees, and I catch a whiff of the sweet, ripening fruit. It reminds me of summer dust and church picnics by the river.

Howly trots over, wagging her tail and sniffing my fingers. She leads us to Jorm. Several branches have swallowed his upper body as he rummages through a mess of leaves. He's still waiting for that growth spurt, hence the stool under his tippy toes.

"Jorm! We're here." Trinna screeches.

Jorm untangles from a branch and points his wire-rimmed glasses at us. This look reminds me of a college professor. I'll never tell him this. Mostly because he'd take it as a compliment.

"You both have to start helping now," he grumbles and returns to rummaging.

"Elbert," whispers a little-boy voice. I turn to Finn. He's smiling with his sweet, tubby face. A mouthful of fruit squishes through his teeth.

If he didn't still wet the bed, he'd be my favorite.

"Hey, Finn." I squeeze the top of his head. "Planning on helping today?"

Finn gives a hearty laugh and shakes his head. "Hmm, no."

I'd be annoyed, but I can't stay mad at that pudgy face. And he knows it. I've already forgiven him five times this week. Five for each time he has scooped up a fire lizard.

He turns to his side and whispers to the air, as if speaking to someone.

"What are you doing?" I ask, even though I know the answer. I was hoping he'd leave his imaginary friend behind today.

"Juni and I are eating peaches," he says.

Jorm pokes his head over and gives a stern look. "Don't talk about her, Finn. Not today."

He's right. Today's not a good day to talk about Juniper.

Finn shrugs and holds a peach to the side like he's helping someone take a bite. "Don't listen to them, Jun-Jun. They're too old to see you."

"C'mon, Finn, I said not today." Jorm's voice cracks. He walks over, snatches the peach from Finn's hands, and throws it.

I give Jorm a dirty look and turn to Finn. His bottom lip is puckering, so I squeeze his shoulder. "We can talk to her tomorrow, buddy."

He lowers his head. "Okay."

We work for a couple more hours, taking breaks to chase down dirt bunnies. The lean, dusty creatures skim the ground with their floppy ears and squirm up trees. Trinna follows one down the length of the grove. She laughs as it tumbles out of reach, but soon her laughter turns to silence.

That's strange. Trinna is never silent.

I glance over. She's inching forward, staring at something in the dirt. "Elbert?" Her voice chills my over-heated bones.

"You okay, Trin?" I ask.

She points to a spot on the ground. "What's that?"

Jorm must have noticed Trinna acting weird because he runs over, Finn close behind. We all peer past her shoulders. I take a minute to recognize what she's pointing at.

They're animal tracks. Large ones. Too large.

"I bet it's Chewbie. She probably got out again," Jorm mutters and turns away.

Chewbie, the friendly cow. She likes breaking through the fence to pay us visits—and chew on our peaches. Or anything else worth chewing.

It couldn't be her. These tracks are much bigger, heavier

—*wilder* than a cow. To make sure, I take a few steps past the trees and peer over at our neighbor's property. As expected, Chewbie is gnawing on the fence, and she's still inside. She glares at me like I should let her out.

"Hey, Chewbs," I call.

She snorts and turns her head. *You're just gonna leave me trapped in here? Some friend.* That's probably what she's thinking right now.

I hurry back to my siblings. "Wasn't Chewbie," I say.

"Oooh. Maybe it was a ghost," Trinna says in a creepy voice. "A giant ghost."

Jorm rolls his eyes. "Ghosts don't leave footprints."

He makes a good point, but Finn is looking pale as a parsnip. I try to lighten the mood. "Maybe it was Finn sleep-walking again. Stop stomping around these parts, Finn."

Finn giggles. "I didn't do this."

While he and Trinna take turns imagining Finn as a giant sleepwalker, I glance at the surrounding peach trees. In one area, the branches are bent and broken off. I lean closer.

"Do you hear that?" Trinna whispers.

I hear it, too. Something is rustling behind us. I whip around and spot tree branches shaking. My throat closes, and I bend my knees, ready to jump in front of the others if need be.

A lanky, freckled arm pushes into the clearing, followed by a boy with squinty eyes. In his other arm, he's holding a pitch-fork, pointy side toward us.

I breathe a sigh of relief. It's only Harold. I should have known it was him, but he was coming from a different way, not from his farm. I would have seen him in his yard with Chewbie just now.

"Where'd you come from, Harold?" I ask. My voice is just above a whisper. I wait for my heart to slow its thumping.

His wild eyes land on me as he grips the pitchfork tighter. "Did anything come by this way?"

Trinna points to the giant tracks. "Are you talking about this?"

Harold walks over, inspecting. "Wow. Even bigger than I thought."

"Did you see something?" I ask.

All eyes are on Harold as he tucks the pitchfork under his armpit. "Yes... By the Upside Down River."

"What was it?" Trinna asks.

"You'll think I'm crazy."

"Tell us!" Finn shrieks, a fierce look on his face.

Harold rubs his forehead. "It was... a giant deer."

"A deer?" says Trinna. "A *deer*?"

I agree. That makes no sense. Also, a little disappointing. I was expecting something more vicious—like a boar, or a grizzly.

"Yup. With antlers the size of an oak tree," Harold insists.

"No way are those deer tracks," I say, siding with Trinna.

The distant clink of a cowbell signals suppertime. My stomach lurches, ready for food, but Harold looks desperate, like he needs someone to believe him. I'm sure he saw something, but Harold's imagination does trick him sometimes. Only last week he swore a sea creature was lazing in the river. Turns out it was a funny-shaped log.

Harold leans close to me. "You gonna tell your pops?"

"I haven't even told him about the fire lizards," I say.

First, we have fire lizards chasing me. Now a giant deer is stealing our peaches.

Some might call this a strange week.

"Just you wait. That deer will come by again. And when it does, I'll be ready," Harold says with a glance at the hills.

"Sure, Harold." Trinna pats him on the back as if he were an old man who's lost his glasses.

Maybe Harold needs glasses.

The cowbell rings a second time.

My siblings and I part ways from Harold and drop off our loads in the storage barn. Thoughts of giant animal tracks slip from my mind, quickly replaced by the savory scents and prospect of a warm meal.

I rush to the washbasin to clean up. The splash of water pinches my hands, sharp like a bee sting. I yank them away and rub my palms with a towel.

"You okay, little brother?" Peto's rumbly voice tickles my ears.

"Have your hands ever hurt after you washed them?" I show him the irritated skin.

"Nah. You'll have to talk to Mom about that one." He glances toward the window. "I think she's out of her room now."

We make our way into the house and gather around the kitchen table. Mom is flushed pink from bending over steaming pots, and her cool gray eyes are splotchy red. Her stout frame dips down today like she's got a weight on her back. Half of her unbrushed hair piles into a bun while the other half sticks to her neck. When her gaze meets mine, her stern mouth relaxes into a dimpled smile, and she points to a chair. "Go on, take a seat, Elby," she fusses softly.

Jorm fidgets at my right while Finn sits to my left with two plate settings. One for him and one for Juniper.

Finn nudges me. "Move, Elbert. You're squashing Juni."

I stare at the space between us, swallow a sigh, and push my chair to the right. That tubby face. Wins every time.

Pops lumbers in, crusty from a long ride in the hills, and creaks into his seat. Everyone falls silent, waiting for him to bless the meal. He knows we're waiting, too. With eyes half-closed, he grips Mom's hand.

"Bless this food and the hearts that prepared it," he says.

"And the ones who harvested," Jorm adds under his breath.

Pops pauses, and Jorm clamps his eyes shut. Then Pops says with the full weight of his voice, "Yes, please bless all of the Dowden family, those who are here, and those who are not."

The emotion in his voice weighs on me, and I stare at my fork while everyone buries their noses into the food. Everyone goes silent—everyone except for Jorm. He's pushing his broccoli around his plate.

"Could use a bit more salt," he says.

"Just be happy you got food," Vida says with a sharp glare.

"I love it," Finn says, and we all smile. Then he points to the space next to him. "Juni loves it too."

All of us, except for Finn, stop moving. I dare to sneak a glance at Pops. His face droops like it usually does whenever someone mentions Juniper, but then he surprises us. He grunts and takes a bite. Between chews, he says, "That's right, Finn. Juniper would love this." He turns to Mom. "Thank you, Moira, for the good food. You too, Vida."

We settle into silence except for the slurping and swallowing of our meal. I'm thinking about Juniper. I'm sure all of us are. Finn may be the youngest this side of heaven, but Juni is the seventh child in our family. Oldest to youngest, we have Vida, Peto, me, Jorm, Trinna, Finn... and Juniper. We had Juniper for just over two years before her life was cut short. Still, she lingers all this time later. Only one of us is comfortable with her memory. Cherishes it, even. And that's Finn.

If only we could be more like Finn.

Trinna clears her throat, cutting the silence. "There's a giant deer eating the peaches. Wasn't Chewbie this time."

Mom blinks at her daughter, then sneaks a glance at Pops. He shrugs.

"Harold saw it. We didn't see it, though," Trinna adds.

"That sounds serious," Mom says in her I-don't-really-believe-you voice.

"Did you see anything in the hills today?" I ask Pops.

He scratches the corner of his mustache. "No. Nothing."

Maybe that's what those tracks were. Nothing. Maybe Harold was just chasing his imagination. If it were anything, it's long gone now. I wish I could have seen it. Whatever it was.

We continue eating in silence. Even Finn eats quietly, pausing between bites to whisper secrets to his invisible sister. Soon, his bottom lip trembles.

"You okay?" I ask.

He cups his hand against my ear and whispers, "Juni's sad."

"Why do you think she's sad?"

He slumps in his chair, thinking. Sometimes I wonder if he understands what happened to Juni just a few years ago. He wouldn't remember the day she died. He was too young. But he can't seem to accept that she's gone—for over five years now. Still, he holds onto her, a memory he's shaped into a friend. A sister.

Finn whispers, loud enough for everyone to hear. "I think she's sad no one wished her happy birthday."

Chapter Three

Peto must have told Pops I've been acting strange lately because he pulls me aside after dinner. "I heard you haven't been feeling well. Something about a candle in your chest?"

I clear my throat, not sure what to say. "Ummm. Sometimes I feel extra hot. On the inside."

He exhales, long and slow, then tilts his face toward the back door. "We'll sleep in the wild tonight."

That's what Pops says whenever he wants to chat with one of us. It's always a special treat, spending a night under the stars, talking to Pops about life and the troubles on our hearts.

While Pops and I spend the next few minutes gathering supplies for a fire, Peto hauls out sleeping mats and wool blankets from the barn. Before settling in, I run to my room and grab a book I'd swiped from Harold, *Call of the Wild*. Harold says it's pretty good. Not because he's read the book—he's still working on his sight words—but more like that's what the shop owner told his mom.

Eventually, everyone but Pops and me retires for the night, and the valley darkens to a murky gray. Pops crouches over the fire pit and knocks flint and steel together. The sparks light the tinder, and soon a blaze is warming our bodies. We relax on our mats and face the deep night. Howly curls up to my right, Pops lounges on my left, and I strain to read by firelight. We're both quiet at first, so I jump a little when he speaks.

"Moon is bright and glistening, huh? Can barely see the stars." He points a toe at the indigo sky.

"Yes, Pops," I say.

He traces his mustache with his thumb and forefinger. "You've been working hard this week. I almost forgot you're a scrappy kid and not a fieldhand working for dimes."

"You gonna pay me, Pops?" I smirk as I toss the idea over.

"You're sharp, Elby. But you know how it works." He says with a snort.

I do know. Somewhere along the way, I understood money is for keeping the farm crawling along while everything else is bought with the sweat off our backs. We split our own wood, darn our own socks, butcher our own chickens, grow our own vegetables and fruits—can those vegetables and fruits, fill our own pails with milk, and so many more things.

But we don't make our own butter. Mom hates churning.

"I need to tell you something," Pops says, interrupting my thoughts.

The tone in his voice raises the hairs on the back of my neck.

Am I in trouble?

His jaw opens again, but no words come out. Not right away.

Finally, he speaks. "It's about your journey to—becoming a man. It's important you understand that as you grow, you'll need to choose who you want to be."

I'm not sure if he's talking about the rising temperatures in my body or the fact water burns my skin, but I wait for him to speak again.

He drags in a breath. "I have an important question for

17

you. I asked Vida and Peto this question around your age, so now I'm asking you."

He waits. My interest bubbles and builds, and finally, I crack. "Okay, what is it?"

He grins. "What future do you wish for?"

I haven't really thought about it, so I say the first thing that comes to mind. "I expect I'll have a wife. She'll probably want kids. Maybe I'll build a home like you did for Mom. I don't know. I want the same as you. An ordinary life."

For some reason, Pops' face darkens and sags.

"Everything okay, Pops?" I ask.

"No. Those are good dreams."

We keep talking after that, but it's mostly me chatting about things like the number of fire lizards I found under the porch today and the fact Finn is afraid of ants. Pops nods his head at the right moments, but his gaze sinks. Is he thinking about Juni?

"You sure you're okay?"

He laughs. Then he sighs and rubs his mustache. "Yes. It's just... sometimes life gets harder before it gets easier. I keep thinking this day will get easier, but..." His voice cuts off.

"But what?"

"No. I shouldn't be weighing you down with this."

"It's okay. You can tell me."

"No." He sets his jaw and stares ahead.

I heed the warning and sit in silence for a bit until I remember why he brought me out here in the first place. We're supposed to talk about what is happening to my body. Am I dying? Or is this normal? I would like to know.

I squash the urge to hold back my next question. "Do you know why I'm feeling so sick?"

Pops shifts back to me, and his eyes soften. "Ah, yes. It happened to me when I was your age. Don't worry. It will pass."

It will pass? That's it?

"So, you felt like a candle was burning in your chest? Water stung your hands?" I feel stupid saying these things, but what if he knows something?

Pops ponders in silence. For a moment, I fear he's dozed off. "Hmm. That is strange."

Not what I was hoping to hear.

"Should I be worried?" I say.

"Of course not. These things happen. Strange things. But it will pass. Just live your life as ordinary, and everything will be okay."

It seems like he should have more things to say, but the way he tightens his arms against his chest and turns his head— I think he's done talking for the night.

"I'm going to sleep now." He nestles into his mat.

"Isn't there more?"

"It's just part of growing up, son," he says with an edge to his voice. Soon, his breathing turns heavy.

I listen to his rattling snores for the next hour and stare at that glistening moon, now almost out of sight. Pops' words linger with me like a bellyache after too many sweets.

It happened to me when I was your age. It will pass.

I scratch at my flushed skin... If what Pops says is true, it should all go away. But when? I don't think he knows what I'm going through. How could he? How could anyone? I've never seen a person's skin turn angry red at the touch of water. I've never seen anyone else shiver against a lukewarm breeze.

Does he really know? Does anyone?

Suddenly, I feel very alone. An anxious feeling hugs my chest and my eyes droop, but not because I'm sleepy. Something sad has settled on me. It reminds me of Pops's face whenever a rainstorm sweeps through town and shutters us inside. Or when Mom pulls out Juniper's tiny yellow dress, the one dotted with strawberries, and holds it to her chest.

But now this sadness belongs to me. I take a while to sort out the meaning of it and why it has arrived so suddenly. And then, I realize that an ordinary life is impossible if I can't shake whatever this is.

This sickness?

No. This isn't just a sickness. This is a *curse*.

Something pokes my side, and I jerk awake. Harold's moonlit face hovers over me as he clutches a pitchfork. Behind him is Chewbie munching on a mouthful of sticks—trespassing again. Judging by the high moon, it's past midnight.

"Uh, hi, Harold."

At the sound of my voice, Chewbie trots over and waits for me to scratch her belly. I oblige, of course.

She grumbles a moo.

"Stop being so nice to her. That's why she's always breaking through the fence and coming over." Harold tries tugging Chewbie aside. She grunts and stays put.

I snort and rub the bottom of her chin. "Why are you up so early?"

"I came to grab Chewbie." He squints at the fields. "Would've let you sleep, but your dog is staring at me. Kinda strange."

I rise to my feet and glimpse Howly in the distance. When she sees me, her head hunches forward and her ears lay back.

"What's she doing that for?" Harold whispers.

She barks up a storm, and my stomach tightens. Howly barks for only one reason—when someone is in trouble.

"Finn," I say. "He's probably sleepwalking." I stoop down to shake Pops. "Wake up, Pops. Finn's gone off by himself again."

He brushes my hand aside. "Of course. I'm coming."

I wait for him to roll to his feet, but he doesn't move.

"I don't think he's awake." Harold says.

"No, he said he's coming. Right, Pops?" I nudge him again.

"I'm coming," he murmurs. Still, he stays put.

"He's just sleep talking. See? His eyes are closed. Must be a heavy sleeper." Harold grips my arm. "If that's Finn out there, he needs us *now*."

He's right. Howly is coming from the direction of the river. If Finn got that far, we might not have much time.

Harold pulls me to my feet, and we race toward Howly. She circles our heels and turns back to the river, and we follow close behind. As we near the stream, I can hear Finn whimpering before I see him. We find him standing in the mud by the water. Clinging to his legs is a family of fire lizards. Fire lizards hate water, and if they get caught wandering too close, they'll do anything to find high ground. In this case, Finn's body. But that won't stop them from spitting on their rescuer.

Howly whines and runs circles. When we get close to the bank, she whines even more, dashing back and forth.

"Finn," my throat struggles to work, "don't move."

Finn looks at us and shivers. "I don't know how I got here."

"That's okay. We're here now." I walk slowly toward him, careful not to spook the lizards.

"Elbert, look." Harold's whisper spooks my insides.

His eyes are fixed on something behind me, further up the stream. I follow his gaze, squinting at a grove of trees. A massive shadow rustles between the branches. My breath catches in my throat, and a ringing slowly fills my ears.

What is that?

"He's here, Elby," Harold whispers. "The beast."

Finn's eyes dart sideways. "Mr. Deer?"

Is that what Finn wants to call him? *Mr. Deer?*

"Don't move, Finn," I say, holding up an arm.

The beast steps out from the trees and into the morning glow. It's a stag with copper fur and a crown of twisting antlers. He's huge—double the size of a draft horse, and he's strolling along the river, his hooves crunching into the gravel. His giant maze of antlers swings toward us and pauses.

Harold swears. "Is he staring at us?"

Finn opens his mouth to scream.

"Finn, don't scream. You'll spook the lizards," I say. I'm feeling helpless now. Any sudden movement could cause the lizards to spit fire.

"I'll go," Harold says. He holds out his pitchfork and moves toward the beast.

"What are you doing?" I call out. "Don't be crazy."

He doesn't answer, he just keeps walking with his pitchfork out. He speaks quietly at first, saying things like, "There ya go, buddy." Then his voice gets stronger. "On you go, big fella."

Finn breathes loudly, no doubt holding in the urge to cry.

"That's good, Finn." I try to soothe him. "You're doing good."

I creep closer and reach for the nearest lizard. Harold bellows, yanking my attention back to him. He's jumped in front of the stag and is waving his pitchfork like a sword.

"Go away," he shouts.

The beast rears his massive antlers and knocks Harold to the ground. Harold rolls until his head slams against a rock. He doesn't move again after that.

The stag shifts toward Finn and me, lowers his head, and charges. I do what a big brother should do. I step in front of Finn and stand my ground.

The beast thunders past rocks and trees, shaking the earth under my feet. Right before he runs me over, the stag twists his antlers and sweeps my legs. My body flings off the ground, and

I crash into something scratchy—a pile of bushes. Rolling sideways, I peer over at Finn.

Is he still moving? Has the stag trampled him already?

No. The stag isn't thrashing or trampling little Finn. He's stooping low, and—

What?

The beast lowers his antlers and gently nudges a fire lizard clinging to Finn's belly. He pushes until the lizard drops off Finn's stomach.

Is he trying to *help* Finn? Does he know Finn is in danger? Because right now, he's removing that danger. One lizard at a time.

Finn quivers, keeping still as the stag continues coaxing each lizard until, one by one, they slide off Finn's arm, his neck, his leg.

Harold stirs awake as the giant creature removes the last fire lizard. Then the beast lifts his head and stares at us one last time. A shock of light explodes from the stag, sharp as a camera flash, and a plume of smoke rolls into the riverbed and swallows us all.

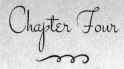

Chapter Four

As the cloud of smoke curls around me, I notice the color—a green tint, and a sparkling sheen. Spooked by the strange dust, the fire lizards scratch their way into the cracks of the earth. My nose burns as a gritty scent rolls over me, and my head teeters like it's full of sand. I keep still, worried that any movement would tip me over. The winds—circling and screeching —stir up dust and river mist.

When the winds dissolve, the stag is gone. In his place, a greenish haze hangs like a ghost above the ground. Something moves in the corner of my eye. I whip around, expecting to see another beast. It's not a beast, but a man, standing at the top of the rise. In the dim light, I can make out the outline of a gray cap and loose-fitting suit. In his hands is an ordinary-looking brown box.

Harold squints. "Who's this guy?"

The man's thumb clenches a knob on the side of the box. Something about it looks familiar. I think I know what that is.

"He's holding one of those portable cameras," I whisper to Harold.

"Mister!" Harold calls. He leaps after the man. "Wait! I want to talk!"

The stranger jumps as if he hadn't noticed us there. He slings his camera over his shoulder, reaches for something in the tall weeds, and yanks a bike to its feet. He hops on and wobbles off without a backward glance.

Harold huffs and springs into a run.

"What are you doing? Harold!"

He'll never catch him, even an old man like that. Not while he's got a bike.

"I'll come by later!" He calls over his shoulder and keeps running.

Normally, I'd be right there with him, chasing mysterious beasts and strangers from out of town, but Finn's pudgy little face is streaked with tears. He is my priority.

"Let's take you home," I say.

Finn quivers. "Am I going to be in trouble?"

As if on cue, Pops bursts onto the scene and squints at us in the dim morning gloom. He barks orders, gruff like a bear. "What are you kids doing out here? Finn? Did you sleepwalk again? Elbert, get Finn home."

I nod and pull Finn along, but Pops grabs me by the shoulder as I walk by.

"Why didn't you wake me up?" he says. There's a bite to his words, an edge in his eyes.

"I tried. I couldn't wake you."

His mouth drops open, clearly in shock. "You should've kept trying. This is not an excuse. You know that. Always wake me up, Elbert."

"I was worried we'd be too late."

Pops blinks, as if breaking from a daze, and a sadness fills his eyes. I've hurt him deeply this time. And now he must be thinking about Juniper.

For her, we were too late.

I choose not to mention the fire lizards that crawled up Finn or the giant deer that disappeared into a cloud of green smoke. Even if Pops believed me when I said a magical beast has been roaming the riverside, as far as I know, that stag has disappeared for good.

As far as I know.

Back at the farm, Finn and I start early morning chores. I can't concentrate, even as I dig into the soil. All I'm thinking about is that giant deer—the way it scraped those lizards off Finn's back. The way it disappeared in a cloud of green smoke.

I wonder how Finn is doing. He was right there next to the beast, staring into its intelligent, piercing eyes. I think he's been gathering the courage to tell Pops what happened, but even he knows this is all too strange.

A giant deer charged into us, saved Finn's life, and then disappeared.

Who'd believe that? Only Harold. Whether he'd been there or not, he would always believe us. I wish I knew where he was now. I doubt he got far chasing that stranger.

And why was that man standing on the hill and taking pictures? Was he like us, just as confused? Or does he know something we don't know?

I hope Harold catches him.

A light finger taps my shoulder, and I flinch, having forgotten where I was for a second.

That's right. I'm in a field digging holes in the dirt, safe from any giant beasts with intelligent eyes. I squint at the owner of the finger. It's Vida. She's holding a bread roll just shy of the tip of my nose. "You thinking about someone, Elby? A lady friend, perhaps? Let me guess. Anne with the auburn hair?"

I reach for the bread, but she tugs back with a smirk. "Well?"

I roll my eyes. "I'm thinking about a girl named Vida. I'm thinking how nice it would be to eat right now. If she'd let me."

"All right, all right. Never mind." She pushes the roll closer to my face, and I grab it and press it to my nose. Still warm. I can smell the tang of sourdough.

Behind her, Trinna bounces between fieldhands, handing out more bread. Most of the workers are temporary hires, immigrants from Japan, brought on to help with the overgrowth of fire lizards and prep for harvest. It's only been a few days, but they seem to know the soil like an old friend, always doing what needs to be done without Pops ever asking. One of the younger ones, a man named Daichi, has been circling the farmsteads of the Salinas valley, hopping from one harvest to the next. Usually, he's elbow-deep in his work, but his eyes keep wandering to Vida's back.

Strange. He must really want a piece of bread.

I raise a hand at the young man. "Hello, Daichi."

He jumps like he didn't notice me there. His charcoal-black hair glistens with sweat, and his cheeks glow red.

"Ah... hello, Elbert," he says quickly. He's quiet as Vida comes over and passes him a bread roll. Instead of heading back to the house, she stays to chat—longer than she should— while Daichi listens to every word. Her eyes sparkle, and Daichi's quiet face gets splotchy red, and that's all they need to have a conversation, I guess.

Everyone works hard today, even with the Salinas Valley winds whipping our backs. By the time I set down my plow, I'm exhausted. I drag my legs off the field and join the fieldhands under the oak tree. Everyone leans over their knees while I lean back and rest my worn-out bones. As a welcoming gesture, Pops invites the fieldhands to share a meal with the family. They agree to stay once they realize Mom and Vida have been cooking all day on their behalf.

When it comes time to eat, we each find a seat—kitchen chairs, upside-down baskets and pails, and blocks of hay wrapped in twine. Most of us are silent, sitting shoulder to shoulder. Then my chest itches. I must have gotten bit by a mosquito at some point—or a spider. I want to examine the bite, but Mom and Vida have already begun passing out plates of food.

The Japanese workers nod their thanks as Mom and Vida hand them a hearty helping of vegetables and chicken. After Pops blesses the meal, we shove food into our mouths. Aside from the fieldhands murmuring their approval, there's a quietness that takes over.

As I fill my body with food, I forget about my itching skin. I settle into the meal and let my thoughts wander into a haze. I don't know what to think right now with this creature prowling the riverbed. I can't be the only one who has seen a giant deer in town. Soon, the rumors will start circling. Soon, everyone will know about this impossibly large deer.

Unless the deer really did disappear.

I take my last bite of food, and it's clear everyone has sunk into a post-dinner daze. Pops leans next to Jorm, whispering something, and my brother races to the house and returns with a violin. He plops the instrument on Vida's lap.

"One song, please," he says.

She smirks and tucks the instrument under her chin. "Okay, then."

She plays a quiet, sad melody. One of the fieldhands hums along, and after a few measures, she lets him take the lead. He forges a mournful melody shaped with words I've never heard before—the Japanese language. The tune is unpredictable to me as he climbs to a high note, then drops suddenly, wavers, and springs up again. His voice is thick, cracking with emotion.

"What does it mean?" Mom asks.

"It's about two loves," Daichi says on behalf of the singer. "My heart loves the soil..." he pauses to translate in his head. "My heart loves my wife in Japan." He keeps glancing at Vida, and a blush swallows half his face.

Some of his kinfolk laugh at him. They must know he's translating their song, but Daichi has no wife, so I'm not sure what's so funny.

Then Daichi says, "Bring my lady home. Bring my lady home. Let her rest on this soil, so I can have both loves again."

The singer hums another tune in the back of his throat, and Daichi and the others join in. Vida rests her bow on her shoulder, listening this time. Their voices swell and break in half. Two parts, a melody and harmony. All of us listening don't dare move or even breathe. We don't want this to end.

When the last note fades, Mom claps her hands, her cheeks glistening. "What does this one mean?"

"It's a call to the Okami, the creature by the river."

Okami? What is that? Did they see Mr. Deer?

"Do you know Okami?" Daichi continues to explain. "The giant wolf creature."

What? A giant wolf? Not a giant stag?

"Giant wolf?" Mom says, sounding amused. "Is that a fairytale from your hometown?"

Oh. That makes sense. Just a Japanese folk story. That's all this is.

"Yes," Daichi answers. "But in Japan, she's just a legend we tell our children. Here, she's real."

I stop breathing for a few seconds. Does this mean there's another giant creature?

"We saw her the first night we made camp by the river. She came out at dusk to guard the hills. When we hum this song, it's like a call. No, like a..." He pauses, searching for the right word.

My scalp prickles. Did we just call this creature? This giant wolf? Is it going to come attack us now?

The warm tickling in my chest bothers me again. I try not to scratch, but I can't help myself. I press my palm against my chest and press down.

"Aha, yes," Daichi says, finding the right words. "The song is like a greeting. We let her know that she's safe with us."

"Safe?" I say. "Why would a giant wolf need to feel safe around *us*? She's the dangerous one."

Daichi lowers his face until the shadows creep into his eyes. "If the Okami is so dangerous, why is she the one hiding from us?"

Chapter Five

By the time the fieldhands retire for the night, my chest has worsened. I excuse myself, run to my room, and unbutton the top of my shirt. I peek down and see something that shouldn't be there. It's not chest hair. Not a freckle. Not a mole. But a feather. A single, red and gold feather, soft like the underbelly of a chicken. And it's growing out of my skin.

What?

I press my fingers against my chest and feel small bumps, like seedlings waiting to sprout. Are there more growing? What will people think when they see that I'm basically turning into a chicken?

Good gravy. Am I turning into a chicken?

A sharp banging on the door makes me jump. On instinct, I button my shirt as fast as I can.

"Just a minute! Don't open the door," I say.

"Elbert? That you?" I recognize Harold's nasally voice.

I let Harold into the room, and right away, I recognize the smirk lighting up his eyes. He's making plans.

"What is it?" I say. "Did you catch up to that man?"

"No, but I've been thinking about it. He might know something."

"Or maybe he doesn't. He was taking pictures like a tourist."

Harold shakes his head. "No, Elby. Tourists don't make long bike trips out to the river at the break of dawn."

He has a point, but it doesn't matter. The beast is gone.

"What's left to do?" I say. "The beast disappeared right in front of us."

Harold's squinty eyes turn buggy. "Oh, lots. Maybe that man knows some things about this creature. Or other odd things. Maybe he's like a mad scientist. Like Dr. Moreau, or Victor Frankenstein, or maybe..." he pauses for dramatic effect, "that beast belonged to him."

I laugh. Harold must be sneaking books from the library again. But he did say one thing that might be worth looking into. *Maybe he knows other odd things.* Maybe he knows something about the wolf creature.

Or boys turning into chickens.

"Did you hear?" I ask. "There's another creature out there. A wolf this time. Big one."

"Another beast! Now we have to talk to him for sure."

He's right. We have to do something. There's still a beast on the loose.

"Okay," I say.

"Great," Harold claps me on the back. "What's the plan then? How are we going to track this guy down?"

"You don't have a plan?" I shouldn't be surprised. Harold gets the ideas. I'm usually left planning out the schemes.

"Not a clue," he says.

I scratch at my chest and think. We need to talk to someone who knows what's going on around town.

Ah, I know. We need Leo Larsson, the town blacksmith— and gossip.

"Let's go see Leo tomorrow. In the morning, before chores."

"Okay," Harold agrees, then leans back on his heels. "But we're sleeping outside tonight."

I shudder just thinking about the sting of night breezes. Last night was bad enough. "Does it have to be outside?"

"Okay, on the porch then. I want to see if any more giant creatures come by. Maybe I'll grab a gun this time."

The spot above my heart burns hot, like a warning. I'm thinking it's good I haven't told Harold about the feathers growing out of my skin. I don't know how he'd react if he heard what's wrong with me. With his imagination, he'd fear the worst.

A sour feeling fills my gut. Is this what it feels like to hide a secret?

"No guns," I say firmly. Harold's mind is too wild for a gun.

"All right. Pitchfork it is."

As promised, Harold joins me on the porch for the night. He stays up late chattering, and he squints into the shadows, looking for the next big creature to cross our path. I keep quiet as I hold on to my secret—my burning chest, my sensitive hands, the fact my skin is sprouting feathers. I wish I could tell him. He'll probably think I'm dying. He could be right.

The grounds hush to silence, including Harold, and true darkness settles in the valley. We're supposed to stay awake and "keep watch" as Harold calls it, but he's already snoozing. Now that I'm wrapped in the dark of night, that hopeless feeling from before creeps back to squeeze my chest. My eyes droop, my mind spirals, and before I know it, I've drifted off.

Like fog rising in the gloom, the Japanese melody saunters into my dreams, and an imaginary rope wraps around my chest. Something or someone has tethered me to the ground. I slog through fields of smoke as my feet suck me back to earth.

I reach through shadows, grasping nothing. I lift my head and wish to fly. But I can't fly.

Not anymore.

The moon climbs above the valley, and the crickets chirp me awake. I've been dreaming, nothing I can remember now, but a tightening in my chest lingers. I glance at Harold. He's got his back to me, still asleep.

A splash of moonlight traces the lawn. Something tugs my chest—a deep need. I have to get off this porch. It's hard to walk softly across the creaky wood, but I manage to tip-toe my way onto the grass and wander toward the garden. I can't explain the feeling that comes next. It's like anticipation, but more than that. Like I'm standing too close to a jagged sea cliff. My arms prickle as I turn the bend to the garden.

I stop. Two figures covered in darkness lean over the rows of vegetables. One is the size of a wagonload of hay but shaped like a wolf—and the other figure is a girl. She whispers to her giant pet and points to a nearby tomato plant. She's holding a repurposed flour sack half-full of something—stolen vegetables, no doubt.

I try to make out the girl's face, but it's too dark. The wolf leans next to her, and she sinks into its shaggy fur until all I can see is a bundle of black hair. The wolf huffs and bends its stout frame, wider than any species of wolf I've ever seen—much like Mr. Deer. A chilling thought pinches me. Does this girl own this monster?

I gather my wits. Should I charge them? Should I spook them off? Is that even possible?

Three bites. That's how long it will take for the beast to eat me.

"Elbert?" Harold stands at the edge of the porch, gripping his pitchfork.

The intruders don't waste a glance our way. The girl leaps onto the back of the wolf, and the two of them bound for the foothills. I chase after them like a dog chasing a pair of dirt bunnies, but these aren't harmless critters. Even now, I don't understand why I'm running toward a wolf the size of a mid-sized elephant. But that rope around my chest tugs me forward, pulling me hard.

Harold catches up to me and yanks me to a stop. "Was that the wolf you were talking about?"

"I think so," I say, straining for air.

He claps me on the back. "We've got another one on the loose, Elbert. That does it. Next time, I'm definitely grabbing my gun."

Chapter Six

Harold and I don't sleep again that night, and by the time the morning fog rolls in, my eyes hurt from staring at every suspicious-looking shadow. No more creatures sneak by, but Harold and I are anxious to dig into the mystery behind these giant beasts. So, before the rest of the family stirs awake, I think of an idea that might give Harold and me an excuse to go into town. I scribble a list of words on a piece of scratch paper, and I wait for Pops to make his morning rounds. As soon as he steps onto the porch, heading for the barn, I run over and hand him the paper.

"What's this?" Pops holds the paper under a patch of sunlight.

"A list of parts we need," I say.

He reads through the list slowly. When he reaches the end, he wrinkles his brow. "When did you make this?"

Early this morning, after realizing the giant beasts creeping through town might be the pets of a girl. Now we need a reason to visit the town gossip, Leo Larsson.

"Well...?" Pops says, prompting me for an answer.

"We made it last night, after working the fields." I hate lying. Thankfully, Pops isn't looking me in the eyes.

He grunts. I interpret this as a laugh.

"Sure," he says and hands the list back to me.

I grab my bike, Harold grabs his. We race down the lane, digging our heels into the pedals as the tires cut grooves into the dirt. With Harold an arm's length ahead, we break into the highway. Horse-drawn wagons lumber past, some loaded with mountains of hay, others with pine crates packed with citrus. A lone, steam-powered automobile chugs bravely along, looking like a distant, weaker cousin of the locomotive. A couple of horse-drawn buggies honk as they creep past.

We roll into town and skid to a halt in front of Leo's Shop. The owner is a lean, grizzled Swedish-American man. He's known for his skill with metal and, more importantly, his gossip. He greets us with a lopsided smile and a tip of his hat. "Hey Harold, Elbert. Good to see you." His voice bends in a twang, a trait carried over from his time spent in the Ozarks. "Elbert, did Pierson send you over for some parts?"

Harold waves the list. "He sure did." He hands the paper to one of Leo's helpers, a boy with soot on his cheeks. We wait for him to the rifle through shelves full of horseshoes, wrought iron poles, hanging leather strips, boxes of nails, and other parts. I lean against the shelf with a copy of a book called *Machines of the 20th Century*—Leo's current read—and a picture of Leo's wife and child. He's never said much about them. I just know they aren't around anymore, but I like Leo's smile in the picture. He's never smiled like that before, not with his eyes all twinkly.

Leo drags his bum leg to my side. "How's life treatin' ya kids?"

"Not much going on," I answer. "Caught Finn sleep-walking again."

He snorts. "How far'd he get this time?"

"All the way to the river," Harold says with a grin.

Leo's mouth gapes before a laugh spills out. "Ha! Well, paint my toenails and call me a china doll. That boy's got a pair of legs, doesn't he? Before we know it, he'll be sleep-walking to the Pacific." A tear drips down the side of the shop owner's soot-smeared face. "But he's okay now? You caught him before he got too far?"

I glance at Harold, not sure what to say. I wasn't planning on giving Leo any gossip today. I was planning on collecting. Finally, I say, "Yes. Yes, we did."

Leo pulls out a wooden pipe whittled in the shape of a bald eagle. Snagging a match from behind his ear, he flicks it against a stray slab of concrete. "Did you see anything while you were out there?"

He holds the pipe out to Harold first, who politely refuses. Then the old shopkeeper turns my way. I shake my head. "No, thanks. Tobacco just doesn't seem healthy to me."

Leo wags his pipe like it were part of his hand. "You could be right, Dowden. I respect your suspicions. But I'm a man of science. I'll wait for the experts to tell me to quit."

I wait for him to take another puff before asking my next question. "Why'd you want to know if we saw something?"

Leo blinks. "Saw something?"

Harold walks over with our bag full of parts. "Yes. Earlier, you asked if we saw anything out by the river."

The old man's blue eyes pop open. He glances around, then leans in with a hushed voice. "Some people have spotted creatures roaming around town. Others found strange-looking tracks."

"Oh, wow." Harold pretends surprise. "What kind of creatures do you think they are?"

"Some say a bear. Others think it's a giant wolf." The shop owner laughs nervously, like he can't believe the words about to come out of his mouth. "Some have seen it disappear into thin air."

Disappear? Who told Leo about the stag disappearing? Did he talk to the man we saw out by the river?

"Who said it disappeared?" I ask.

Leo glances down and squints, trying to remember. "Uh, Halifax, I think his name was. He's just visiting. He's a photographer from San Francisco."

"A beast disappearing, huh?" Harold shakes his head like he doesn't believe a word. Good strategy. The more we disbelieve Leo, the more he'll say.

The blacksmith laughs, and then he sighs. "Okay, okay, I'll say it. I was sitting on my porch, watching the sunrise, when a creature lurked past my property, a giant shadow the size of a black walnut tree. I hollered at it. And then it disappeared. Right in front of my eyes."

Harold shakes his head. "That's crazy talk, Leo."

Harold's right. This rumor sounds impossible, fantastical —almost *superstitious*. But it must have been hard for Leo to share something like this.

Then, as if to prove my thoughts, Leo says, "I may be a man of science, but I'll say, seems like we've got *magical* creatures on our hands." A wave of fear fills his eyes, as if saying the words out loud made them truer than before.

"You okay, Leo?" I ask.

He grabs my wrist and Harold's shoulder. "You boys be careful. Don't go out alone. It's dangerous out there."

Something about the way he says this, it's like he knows something else. "You think they're dangerous?" I say.

He tightens his lips and nods. "I come from the Ozarks. They've got stories about beasts like these. I never thought I'd see any out here. Never really completely believed. But now..."

39

I understand Leo's reluctance to believe. I, myself, didn't believe until I saw the beasts with my own eyes.

I'm not sure how to say this next part smoothly, so I just blurt it out. "Is Mr. Halifax still in town?"

Leo turns to me and narrows his eyes. "Yes, he is. Why do you want to know?"

My mouth stops working. I don't have a lie ready on my tongue.

"We want to talk to him," Harold steps in. "We think he might know more about these giant beasts."

It's times like these that I'm grateful for Harold. He says just enough truth, we don't need to lie.

"I don't suppose you know where he's lodging?" I say.

Leo's eyes probe me like a poker to a fire. "Riverside Hotel over in Hilltown."

Harold glances at me and nods.

Time to go.

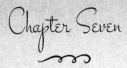

Chapter Seven

Harold and I drop off our supplies at the house and ride back to the main road toward Riverside Hotel. I crank the pedals and lean into the blustering wind, angling for the fork in the road. The canvas layer of my rubber tires sweeps the ground, veering me left.

We glide down a road etched with wheel tracks and horse-shoe markings, and I swerve to avoid a dip in the ground. We pass a white picket fence and skid to a halt in front of the Riverside Hotel. A neighborhood mutt trots over and growls at me. I'm used to sidestepping ratty-looking dogs, so I don't think much of it, but Harold tugs me to his side.

"Careful, Elby," he says. "That one's not right." He points to the froth spilling over the animal's teeth.

That's not good. Someone will have to put him down before he attacks someone. I wait for the mutt to turn down the alley, then I spring forward, straight for the hotel. I reach the front door and open it, revealing a dusky, dark saloon. The clinking of glass and murmurings reach my ear as I head for the lobby with Harold lumbering behind.

Harold waves at the barkeep tucked in the corner.

"Oh, hi Harold. Hi Elbert." The barkeep is Conor, a friend of Harold's. Conor points to a shelf of toe-curling liquors and murky glass cups. "Care for a drink?"

Harold smirks like he's had many drinks in his time. "That's okay, Conor. We're just here to meet a friend. Also, we've got a rabid mutt roaming the street. Think you could send someone after it?"

Conor nods at a young man in the corner and points to the exit. "Andrew, go see if there's a mangy dog in the alley." He turns back to Harold. "Another one? That's not good. Yeah, Andrew will take care of it."

I clear my throat. "Erm... is Mr. Halifax around?"

A half-smile lingers on Conor's face. He's got thoughts swirling in those eyes. Do we look suspicious? I hope we don't look suspicious.

"I see," Conor says. "Well, normally I'd go knock on his door, but I'm not supposed to leave the counter just yet. Not until Andrew gets back from taking care of that dog."

Harold crinkles his brow. "You sure there's nothing you could do? It's pretty important."

Conor shrugs. "Ah, okay. Well, let's just see..." He grabs a sheet near his elbow. "Mr. Halifax. Room 209."

That's all I need to know. I toss a "thank you" over my shoulder and hurry toward the stairs. I don't wait for Conor to stop me.

I take the stairs two at a time, and then I slow at the last couple of steps, just short of a corridor bathed in shadows. The stench of unwashed bodies seeps through the walls, and the whistling winds slide past the windows. Sucking in a breath, I step into the darkness.

Room 209 is at the end of the hall on the right. I lean my ear against the wooden door and wait for the pulsing in my head to slow down. All I hear is the wind thumping against the shutters. Or is this my heart chugging in my chest?

I lift a hand and notice something new. Three more feathers curl around my wrist. With my arm outstretched, they've peeked past the cuff of my shirt. My nerves fire as I pat my chest, probing the skin. My fingers trace more feathers— small, but they're growing. I find a few more under the nape of my neck.

This is getting worse. How much longer can I hide this? Soon, the instinct to hide won't matter. I'll have no choice. But I don't have time to worry. I'm steps away from the stranger.

Tension builds behind my fist. I knock. Softly at first. Not even a mouse would hear. I knock again. Louder.

Nothing. No creaking steps, no shuffling of papers, no sigh, and no one calling out "who's there?"

"Mr. Halifax?" I whisper just above the wind and press my ear back to the door. I clasp the wrought iron handle and lean.

The door cracks open, and my heart jumps. Deep down, part of me knows stepping into this room without permission is wrong. But I've come this far. I'm not going back now.

With the door cracked open, I half expect Mr. Halifax to leap from a corner and attack me. After all, I'm the intruder. But the room is empty. All that occupies is a cot piled with a mountain of blankets, a cracked-open suitcase, and—

A shiver runs up and down my spine. In the corner is a table piled with papers and columns of books. And above that table is a growing collection of photographs tacked to the walls in neat columns. I force my legs to the table. Several of the book titles are familiar: *The Island of Doctor Moreau* by H.G. Wells, *Frankenstein* by Mary Shelly, and *Alice in Wonderland* by Lewis Carroll. I've read all of these stories, and each of them has supernatural or fantastical characters. Some characters are human-like animals, or animal-like humans, while other characters are mad scientists. Like Harold suspected Mr. Halifax to be.

Then I find *The Encyclopedia of Mythical Creatures* and *The Almanac of Strange Peoples*. I flip through the almanac first. It's filled with odd-looking people, including twin girls with bodies attached at the hip, men with fur wrapping their skin, and a girl the size of a china doll standing next to a man as broad as a draft horse.

I could be one of these people. The thought chills me. How many of them grew into their oddities the way I am? How many of them overcame their sickness? Their curse?

My hand brushes over *The Guidebook to Mexican Folklore*.

Interesting. I wasn't expecting this.

I flip through the pages and stop at a chapter that's been underlined three times: *The Shapeshifter of Mexico.*

Shapeshifters? And that stag...

A flash of realization tingles in my chest. The stag did not simply disappear. He changed shape. Into a *human?* But I didn't see—of course. The green smoke. It blinded me. Confused me. This must be his way to distract us and escape. Well, it worked.

My hands shake as I sift through the chapter, pausing at the images inked between words. One picture is of a wolf, one of a stag, a crocodile, a dog, a jaguar, a mountain lion. I scan further. Part of me wonders.

Am I like them?

I finish scouring the list of animals, but I do not find my creature listed. No chicken. No bird with orange and yellow feathers. No creature that burns with fire and fears water.

My hands dart to the loose papers jumbled across the table. Most of them are newspaper clippings with headlines that say things like "Giant Wolf Sightings," "Crocodile in the Upside Down River," and "Big, Friendly Buck Visits Chualar."

How many of these shapeshifters are there? How many towns are they inhabiting? Panic surges through me, and my mind wanders into the dark. I clench my jaw and reel in my wits.

Breathe. Calm yourself.

I take deep breaths, forcing air down my lungs until my arms stop tingling. This is getting stranger by the minute. Makes me wish Harold were here.

Where is he, anyway?

I glance at the wall covered in photographs. A new wave of nausea spills through my body, and I grip the table to steady myself. There, at eye level, is a picture of me. I'm standing next to Finn, and just beyond us is a pillar of smoke. A faint shadow darkens part of the haze. A human shape.

There's my proof. Mr. Deer didn't vanish. He *changed shape*.

My eyes move to a different picture of a dark shadow blotting out a grove of trees. Is that the wolf? Next to that picture is one of the rippling Salinas river. I glimpse a faint outline of something hulking in the shallows.

Crocodile.

Above that is a photograph of the Gabilan range, and in front of those mountains, stooping down for a bite of grass, is the shadow of the stag. Next to that is a picture of a young girl. She leans over the swift river current, reaching toward something in the water. A bundle of dark hair trails down her back.

I lean to get a better look, and my toe bumps against something hard. I reach under the table and pull out a camera. *The* camera. It's the portable one Mr. Halifax used to snap these photos.

I glance over everything—the camera and photographs, the textbooks, the newspaper clippings, and the growing village of images tacked to the wall—and I realize something. Mr. Halifax is not a tourist.

"Hello?" a groggy voice mumbles in the corner.

I jump back and face the mountain of blankets piled on

the cot, and my stomach drops. That's not a pile of blankets. There's a body under a mass of covers.

The soft face of Mr. Halifax stares back at me. He bolts upright in his cot, speechless.

I open my mouth, but no words come out. He must think I'm here to steal from him. He's going to call for help any second. I should have knocked harder. I should have waited for permission to enter this room.

Before either of us muster any words, the door bangs against the wall. In strolls a lanky freckled boy with a grin on his face.

Chapter Eight

"Hello, good sir." Harold stands as if he's stood in this room many times. "My name's Harold, and I see you've met our groundskeeper, Elbert. Don't mind him. He's just here to tidy up the room. Elbert, Conor wants us working the dining hall now..."

"What? Groundskeeper?" Mr. Halifax waddles off his bed in his nightshirt. He reaches for a pair of trousers. "A groundskeeper tends outside a building, not inside someone's room—uninvited."

Harold doesn't waver. His confidence seems to grow as he digs deeper into his lie. "Yes. Elbert mentioned he'd left a few tools in here..."

Now properly clothed, the irritated look on Mr. Halifax's face melts into something worse—anger. He points a finger at Harold. "Now, look, boy. I don't know why you're spinning these lies, but you might as well come out with the truth." He turns his round, gray eyes to me.

Harold sighs. "Okay, I'll be honest."

Oh no. This can't be good.

"I was just saying those things because I'm not sure if

Elbert wants to ask you some questions about that giant stag we saw, or if he wants to get out of here," Harold says with a shrug.

Mr. Halifax holds up a silencing hand, and the stern pinch of his brow softens. He blinks like he's seeing me for the first time. I tug on the cuff of my shirt just in case any feathers are poking out.

"Questions?" He looks at Harold. "Was that you by the river?"

I take a step forward. "Yes, sir. We were there when the stag disappeared. And we've seen the other beast—the wolf roaming town." I take a breath, giving him time to react. He says nothing, so I go on. "We thought you might know something."

A light flashes in the man's eyes, followed by a look of surprise, and then his face changes from confused to curious. "You could've just asked."

He strides over to his desk and shuffles through news clippings. "Rumors have been circling up the coast about these beasts, all the way to San Francisco, but only certain papers will publish any reports. I recently tracked them here. There are three of them—a stag, a wolf, and a crocodile. They seem to know each other." He points to the photo of the girl next to the stream. "And then there's this girl. She isn't like them. Maybe one day she'll be able to shapeshift. Not sure. I haven't figured her out yet."

Harold scratches the back of his head. "Shapeshift?"

Mr. Halifax grins. All traces of anger have left his face. "Yes. Shapeshifters. People who can change from human to animal." He holds up an article dated thirty years ago. "Look here. I found this in the *San Francisco Tribune* archives." He taps a photo of a man standing next to a giant dog with intelligent, glowing eyes. "We've had these shapeshifters for years— decades. Most of the time they lay low, keep to themselves, but every once in a while they come back around and show themselves, usually briefly, before they disappear again and fall back into myth."

Harold's face is a new shade of white. "How dangerous are they?"

The man's bushy eyebrows jump to his hairline. "Oh. Well, shapeshifters are people just like you and me. Are they dangerous? Depends on the person. Just like anyone else. If they're evil, they'll do evil things. If they're good, they'll do good things. These ones haven't caused any harm that I know of."

"Okay. So, you have no idea," Harold says. "And they can be anyone? They look just like us?"

"I'm still researching. But yes. That's how it seems," says Mr. Halifax.

I step in with a question of my own. "Why do you think the girl is going to change like them? She's ordinary. Maybe she'll stay that way." I try not to scratch at my prickling skin, a reminder that I am *not* ordinary.

"That's right," Mr. Halifax says. "She could become like them. As far as my research shows, this ability to shapeshift is passed on to others. But I'm not sure how that works."

I pause for a minute. Isn't it strange that this lone man is chasing a myth of shapeshifters? Why would he do this? I give him a hard glare. He doesn't seem to notice me scrutinizing him as his round face tweaks into a smile and his curvy mustache tickles his cheeks.

"Fascinating, isn't it?" He says.

He's a curious man, but he could be dangerous, not only to these shapeshifters. He could be dangerous to *me*. "What do you plan on doing to these people, Mr. Halifax?"

The urge to protect these shapeshifters stirs inside me. Something about them—their strangeness—feels familiar. Maybe I'm not really protecting them. Maybe I'm protecting myself. What would this man do if he knew how strange I am?

Mr. Halifax's face opens in surprise. "Oh, no! Oh, I would never hurt these wonderful, magically gifted people. Call me an observer. I'm here to learn from afar. I'm a researcher. I want to fill this book." He grabs *The Shapeshifter of Mexico* book and waves it in front of us. "I want to fill in the gaps of shapeshifter lore. It's fascinating because many cultures around the world have humans who can change into animals. It's a magic no one understands. I want to understand it. I want to find the common thread—even if I'm the only one who believes it."

I'm not totally convinced, but the way he speaks, I believe he means no harm to these people.

That doesn't mean he's harmless.

Harold rubs his face with his hands and winces.

"Are you okay?" I ask.

He shakes his head. "No, this is so much worse than I thought. Three shapeshifters prowling around. Maybe even four. What are they planning on doing? How are we going to get rid of them?"

This is the first time I'm noticing how much fear has taken over Harold. Has he felt this way the whole time? I can't believe I didn't see this before. I thought he was just curious, searching out an interesting mystery to solve. But he's been planning to destroy the only people who might understand what's happening to me. Before I know it, he'll be chasing *me* with a pitchfork.

My insides churn and my face flushes red. I must hide what's happening to me. But how can I? Soon Harold will see the feathers poking out of my skin. He'll be as afraid of me as he is of these strangers. What will he do then?

Just the thought makes the fire in my chest swirl faster. My arms tingle, and soon the feeling travels to the tips of my fingers. Mr. Halifax and Harold turn to me, staring. Harold's mouth pops open, but for once, he's lost for words.

My instincts take over, and a warning blares in my mind.

Hide. Run. Hide.

I bend my knees, planning my route of escape.

"Wait." Harold's sharp voice stops me short. He grabs my sleeve.

Oh no. He's going to see what's wrong with me. He's going to know I'm a monster.

A storm rumbles in my gut as my best friend tugs back my sleeve and examines the violet-orange feathers poking through my skin. Slowly, a red flush takes over his face, and a new fear darkens his eyes.

I try to laugh, but nothing comes out. "I might be turning into a chicken."

"Elbert? You're a... shapeshifter?"

Just the idea sends a fresh wave of panic to my chest. Heat gathers inside my fists, and pressure pushes against my fingertips.

Is that what I am? A shapeshifter?

"I don't know," I say. It's the truth.

"You don't know?" His confusion heats to anger. "But you knew *something* was happening. Why've you been hiding this from me? I tell you everything."

"I don't know," I lie.

I still can't bring myself to tell him everything—about the sickening warnings that blare in the back of my mind, even now that everything is in the open. The truth is, I don't trust him. And he knows it.

I might as well have pushed him off a cliff.

"I can't believe that's your excuse," he says. "That you don't know."

A cold warning grips my gut, telling me to be careful. I shouldn't share anything else.

What's left to hide? He's seen the worst, hasn't he? But he could turn against me. He already has. I can see it in his eyes, this deep-seated fear, like I've abandoned him. He can't even look at me now.

"It just started happening," I say. "Pops says I should ignore it, and it will go away."

So far, no luck with that.

Meanwhile, the spinning heat builds in my chest, and that pressure pushes hard against my fingertips. It makes me nauseous. I can't hold it in anymore. And I do something I've never done before. I open my hand and a spark bursts from my palm.

It lands on Harold's shirt.

Chapter Nine

Harold jumps back and yelps like a dog. He pats down the glowing spark before it grows into a flame. Halifax hops over to help Harold snuff out the ember, and once the shirt is all but smoking, the man glances up. A look of delight and fascination shines in his eyes. "Did you just light that on fire?"

I look at my palms, a little pink, but no other signs of having thrown fire. If I didn't know better, I'd say I imagined it. A wave of shock numbs me, and there's the horror on Harold's face, his wild eyes pinned on me. He stares as if I've morphed into a giant beast. In a way, he's right.

He points a finger and opens his mouth, but nothing comes out. I've scared him speechless. I've never seen Harold speechless. It doesn't matter. I can see it on his face. I'm a stranger to him now, a creature to be feared. All traces of friendship have slipped from his eyes.

I press my arms to my sides, hoping the flames in my body stay put. They don't. Another spark drops from my other hand and lands on the rug. I skid backward, toward the door.

"Please don't say anything." My voice aches because I know it's pointless to ask. "Don't tell anyone."

I turn from them and run. I stumble down the hallway and push past an open window, and a gust of icy wind rams into my burning body. Just before I reach the stairwell, the fire inside me calms to a whisper. I breathe easily again until I hear heavy footsteps.

"Come back, Elbert! Don't go!"

I leap for the stairwell, ignoring Harold's shouts. But that wasn't Harold's voice. That was Mr. Halifax. No, Harold won't want me to come back. He probably never wants to see me again.

Should've stayed hidden. Shouldn't have asked so many questions.

The doubts sting, but I'm too distracted with things like forcing myself not to cry and walking past Conor without getting stared at by half the room. I push open the double doors leading to the street and gasp for air. Was I holding my breath this whole time?

I leap onto my bike and crank the pedals. Already, tears are burning the corners of my eyes. I ride straight for the farm even though, deep down, it doesn't feel like home anymore. Homes are supposed to feel safe. A place I can share my secrets and doubts and get answers about things I don't understand.

This—I don't understand. No one understands, and that lonely feeling comes back stronger than before. It hurts to realize this, but I can't tell anyone. I have to keep this to myself.

So, I wipe the tears from my eyes, and I hold in my secret, no matter how painful it feels. I slide my creaky bike to its resting place by the barn and shuffle past Pops and Peto, Jorm and Trinna and Finn, Mom and Vida, saying nothing. I finish the day as if nothing happened. Every second feels like a minute, and every minute feels like an hour.

Finally, the sky fades to black, and I sink into my bedsheets and close my eyes before Finn has time to ask for a bedtime story. Tonight, I need to be alone. Tomorrow, I'm not sure I get to hide anymore.

I brave the next few days, expecting Harold to have shared with the whole town he's got a monster for a best friend. That's assuming we're still friends. He hasn't spoken to me since I burst into flames. I tip-toe around Mom and Pops, expecting them to say something, or at least call for Doctor Brownly to examine me. They don't say anything. And neither do my siblings.

I've gotten good at hiding the feathers sprouting on my arms and chest, and some have traveled down my legs. I wear long sleeves and pants, and I've started wearing work gloves. One morning, I notice a red sheen in my hair, so now I'm wearing a hat at all times. Everyone wants to know how I can stand the heat.

"I don't mind," I tell them. And it's true. I welcome anything warm. Any excuse to shield me from the breeze.

Every night, I'm the first to retire to bed. Every morning, I'm the last to wake. I refuse to change clothes around my brothers, and I cover my face with a hat when I can. It's easy to hide around family. Everyone knows what I look like. They're not expecting any changes, so no one looks at me closely. Not even Vida. I think she's finally given up on her quest to get me to admit I'm in love with Anne with the auburn hair.

The month of June is nearing the end, and the sugar beet fields have been picked clean. Soon Pops will start tilling the soil again and prep the rows for planting. With the bulk of the harvest over, the fieldhands have packed up and headed north for corn picking. One of the older fieldhands has signed on as a tenant farmer for Spreckels, the large beet factory down the road. Daichi plans to join him. They've already chosen a second crop to cultivate—strawberries.

Meanwhile, no one has confronted me about my body changing. Maybe everyone's too distracted to notice, or maybe Harold did as I asked. He's keeping my secret. At least for now. Or maybe he's waiting for me to do something bad. Then he'll have a reason to tell on me.

And what will he do about the shapeshifters? What *can* he do? Spook them off with a pitchfork? Unlikely.

I'm pretty sure the girl and her wolf have continued sneaking onto our property at night. I must be sleeping more deeply than usual because I never hear anyone creeping on the grounds, but Peto is convinced someone stole glass jars from the barn, and Vida swears the wildflowers by the porch have been snipped to stubble. She blames Jorm. Jorm blames me. I blame the wolf.

I wish I were a lighter sleeper. Then I could have caught them in the act. Especially since last night was different. Last night, the girl didn't take vegetables and peaches from us. Instead, she left something behind.

Mom finds it first—a new plant growing in our garden, a plant we haven't grown for years. Strawberries. We used to grow them, but that was *before*, when we were living in Arkansas. We haven't grown them since, well, not since Juniper was around.

But I remember...

I remember pulling the fruit from their stems and holding them against my lips. Mom would tell me to look at the tops. "If it's red, that means they'll be really sweet," she'd say. Her eyes were softer back then.

And Juniper would be there, crawling into the strawberry bed like she was returning to a favorite blanket. She'd stretch out her hand, reach for the fruit, and jam one into her mouth, along with a couple of fingers. Then she'd giggle, her syrupy-brown eyes twinkling.

I remember the sharp change after she was gone, especially those first few months. Mom slowed down. It took great effort for her to start something, even simple tasks like boiling a pot of water or drawing her face into a smile. Pops was unlike the rest of us. He grew bigger and stronger, as if grief stoked a fire in his bones. He built our home in just a few short months. I believe a fire still drives him now. I wonder what would happen if he ever slowed down.

He and Mom fought at night about things I could only guess about, so Peto and Vida started tucking the little ones into bed. Back then, I was one of "the little ones." I let them do it without a fuss, but Jorm squealed, demanding his *real* parents. After a while, even he came to accept this new ritual. During serious moments, like the fighting between parents and the death of a sister, the kindness of siblings is sacred.

A patch of strawberries this late in the season could be a coincidence, or it could have been put there on purpose. Either way, I'm anxious to know what Mom plans to do with them. I won't blame her if she tears them out and throws them on the compost heap.

"I'll take them out if you want," I say.

"No, Elbert. We're keeping them."

She says this on the last day of June.

Now that June has ended, we can breathe again. It's time to tuck Juniper's memory into the back of our minds until this time next year. July is here, and Pops is back to his grueling schedule, lightening our load of chores, and Mom is fussing and poking around the house again. I'm running out of ways to hide the feathers crawling up my face, and Pop's words don't seem so wise anymore.

It's only a phase. It will pass.

As a new growth of feathers blossoms behind my left ear, I'm starting to think Pops has no idea what he's talking about.

Chapter Ten

Today is the fourth of July church picnic, which means we need to rush through morning chores.

Peto and I start by pruning the orchard—after shooing Chewbie back to her side of the property, of course. Meanwhile, Vida locks herself in the kitchen to bake her famous blackberry pies. A couple of our neighbors stop by to help Pops haul a new load of peaches from the storehouse onto the wagon. When Pops returns from the loading station, we rush to our rooms and change into our Sunday best. I, of course, wait for my brothers to change first before throwing on a light blue buttoned shirt with extra-long sleeves.

It takes everyone a few minutes to get ready, except Vida. She's piling her hair on top of her head in the shape of a mushroom.

"What do you think, Elbert?" She plumps her hair and twirls in her new lavender skirt. Cream gloves cover her hands. A bit warm for summer. That's fashion, I guess.

"Daichi will love it," I say, smirking.

Vida halts. A wave of red splotches her cheeks and races down her neck.

"Elbert!" She chases me with her brush and swipes at my head.

I dash to the living room and around the entrance hall. That's where I stumble onto Daichi. He's wearing a carefully pressed cream sack suit. A red bowtie nestles under his chin, and his hair is combed neatly to the side. He grips a straw hat in one hand and clenches a fistful of wildflowers in the other.

"Hello there, Elbert." He shoves his hat under his armpit and reaches for a handshake.

I expect his slender hand to be flexible and soft. Instead, his shake is firm and unyielding. I meet his gaze, and his eyebrows bunch together. A glow warms the deep brown pools of his eyes.

"Hello, Daichi. How're the strawberries?"

Daichi breaks into a smile. "They're good, Elbert. They're just seedlings right now. Won't be ready for planting until after winter."

That's right. I still don't know who planted those strawberries in our garden. "I've got a strange question for you," I say.

His cheeks turn cherry red, and his eyes dart to the side. "Um... question? You mean, about your sister?"

"Who, Vida? No, not her. I was wondering about the strawberries growing in our garden. They just appeared one day. Did you plant some for us?"

"Oh, no Elbert." He shakes his head. "I don't know anything about that."

"That's too bad. I wonder who it is then."

"Vida." Daichi steps past me. His mouth slides open as he takes in Vida's cushion-shaped hair and white leather gloves.

"I told you he'd love it," I say.

This time Vida turns red as a sunburn. Vida launches her brush at me. I duck too late and get clocked in the forehead.

Mom barges into the room with Finn and Trinna

stomping at her ankles. She halts, greets Daichi, then herds us out the door.

Daichi and Vida take our smaller horses, Mits and Bits, while Fuzzy Lips hauls Mom, Pops, and the youngest ones in the wagon. Peto and I take the bikes. Dust puffs like steam behind our wheels, a sign of how thirsty the earth is. Peto whoops as we near the riverbank. It's already swarming with frolicking children, women balancing platters of food, and men lugging sheets and baskets. One man leans against a log like he's been there for hours. He balances an accordion on his knee and sings a tune about a man who can walk through fire. His voice bobs at the end of each verse, the accordion humming along.

He sets his sights on a woman born without a silver spoon,
Her eyes of fire melt the hearts of all her beaus
But only one man braves the flames.

After parking my bike, I wade through the blond grasses, brittle from the dry season. Star thistles prickle my ankles as I kick my way to a clearing. I pass Leo, who's sitting on a boulder closer to the river. He's chatting with Pops. Strung around the blacksmith's neck is a pair of binoculars. He catches me staring, so he holds up the device and grins. "Made these so I can spy on the beast," he says. "Just in case it shows up."

I notice a long sheath strapped to his waist.

"Will you be attacking giant wolves with that sword, Leo?" I ask.

He glances at the blade and then at his bum leg. Smirking, he says, "You doubt my abilities, Elby? If he's going downhill, I could tuck and roll, fast as anyone."

"Oh, no, Leo. Sorry, I didn't mean to offend you."

He laughs until his eyes squeeze shut. "Don't worry, boy. I

don't offend easily. Actually, I prefer to do the offending, when I get the chance."

"Okay then," I say with a grin. I walk closer, keeping my hat tucked low, so he can't see the feathers behind my earlobes. "Did you make the sword?"

He tightens his mouth, sobering. "Of course, I did. For protection. We've had some recent attacks."

A chill sweeps through me. Attacks? I thought Daichi said this was a peaceful beast. Mr. Halifax said so, too.

"Who's been attacked? Are they okay?"

"No, not attacks on people. On animals. Some dogs have gone rabid."

I remember the mutt outside Riverside Hotel. "But that's nothing new. Animals catch rabies sometimes."

"Ah, but right now? Right when this creature arrives? Looks suspicious if you ask me."

I shrug, not wanting to encourage him. "I don't know, Leo. Shouldn't we get more scientific evidence to back up this idea?"

At first, he looks at me like I've slapped him, then slowly his face bends into a smile. "Well, roll me in a blanket and call me a piglet. You're right, Elby. Too bad no one's been able to catch one." He holds up his binoculars. "Guess I'll keep on lookin' out for 'em. Maybe we'll get lucky one of these days."

This is not the reaction I was hoping for, but at least he's moved away from accusing the shapeshifters of spreading rabies. If Leo says something, his word will travel around town. I'm sure it already has.

"Go on now," Leo gently pushes my shoulder. "You don't need to talk to an old man like me. Look, there's Harold."

I glance back, and the first thing I notice is not Harold but a girl wearing a cream dress. She grips her straw hat as loose auburn curls trail down her back. It's Anne, the girl Vida is convinced I've been thinking about these past couple of days.

She's talking to Harold, my former best friend, now possible enemy. Resting at their ankles are some paddle boats. Harold is gesturing to one of them.

I still remember Harold's face the last time I saw him, ghost-white with fear. As I glare at him square in the face, he glances back. His eyebrows raise, most likely surprised I've joined this public gathering, then he squints, no doubt suspicious of my gloves and low-hanging hat. All traces of friendship are gone from his eyes.

Vida steps close and bumps my elbow. "Are you going to talk to her?"

I roll my eyes. "Goodbye, Vida."

Vida winks like she knows everything and slides back into the arms of Daichi. They stroll toward the river, neither one aware of the probing looks of church members.

I walk over to Harold and Anne and tip my hat. "Good afternoon."

Harold jerks back like he touched a hot pan. "Why are you here, Elbert?"

Anne shoots him a surprised look. "Why would you say that, Harold? Of course, he should be here." She smirks and crosses her arms. "Haven't seen you at church in a while, Elby."

"Yes, I know," I say. "It's always hard to be around crowds this time of year."

Anne's sea-green eyes glimmer, and she reaches for my arm. I resist the urge to flinch away. I hope she doesn't notice how hot my skin is right now—or the feathers poking through the fabric of my shirt.

"I'm sorry," she says. "I wish I'd met your sister."

I believe her. Many have told our family this. "It's okay. It's July now. The hardest part of the year is over."

She grins, but Harold stares like he's got iron pokers for eyes. I clench my fists and stomp down the urge to slink away.

He looks so cold, but I have to talk to him. I have to know if he's going to share my secret. "Um, Harold. Do you have a minute?"

He blinks like he can't believe I'd ask such a question. "No."

His quick response stings, and my heart crumples. Anne must have noticed because she tries to distract us. "We've got three paddle boats here. Want to race?"

"Yes," I say, without thinking.

Anne turns to Harold, all smiles and rosy cheeks. "Well, Mister? Are you going to join us?"

I'm starting to like Anne more—as a friend, of course. She really wants Harold and me to get along. Thanks to her sweet glances, Harold's freckled ears turn pink, and he agrees.

"Okay," he says. "One race."

Anne pushes her boat into the northbound waters of the Upside Down River. Harold quickly follows suit. Then, as I approach the muddy banks, I remember that water brings me pain. Lots of it. Maybe this is a bad idea.

Too late now.

I squelch into the mud, pushing the boat from the river-bank to the water. I'm grateful to have boots protecting my feet. If I were barefoot, I'd be writhing in pain right now. I hop into the boat, almost too soon, and I bob for a bit, hung up on some rocks. I break free when I push my paddle against the bottom of the river.

We try our best to line up our boats, and Harold points to an unusually shaped log farther upstream and dubs it the finish line. This reminds me of the time he swore he'd seen a crocodile lounging in the river. I wonder if that's what he'd seen. With all these strange things happening, I wouldn't be surprised if he'd been right.

Anne and I agree the log is our destination, and on the count of three, we're off.

We start with an even pace. Anne is focused. I know she is cooking up a strategy while Harold and I huff along. I give her space to inch ahead, and she takes it, jamming her oar into the water. Harold pokes his oar like he's spearing for fish.

"Harold," I whisper over to him, quietly so Anne can't hear, "we have to talk."

Harold shakes his head. "No, we don't. I'm not talking to you."

"Have you told anyone about me?" I force out the words. I hate asking this, probably because I'm afraid of what the answer will be.

"No need," he says. "Townsfolk will find out soon enough. Besides, no one would believe me."

This, sadly, is most likely true. If anyone believed Harold's wild imagination, it was me, and usually only me.

Behind his shoulder, I glimpse a shadow rippling in the reeds. A very large shadow.

A cold feeling grips my stomach. Could it be another shapeshifter? Is it the wolf prowling the riverbed?

A dark thought comes to me. What does a giant wolf eat for food? Boys like me?

The shadow rustles close to the riverbank, but Anne and Harold don't notice. Anne has pulled far ahead now while Harold and I continue rowing side by side. Both of them have fixed their eyes on the finish line.

If I'd been paying attention to Harold and not the shadow slinking between trees, I might have noticed the oar inching toward me. Suddenly, a harsh knock forces my boat into a wobble.

"What are you doing?" I yell as I dig my oar into the current, trying to level out.

Harold lets out a nervous laugh and swings his oar for my head, not too hard, so he can say he was playing, but hard enough to throw me off balance. I teeter against the wrinkled waters.

"I don't want you following us," he says. "I don't trust you."

He looks sad, like he can't be friends with me anymore.

"I'm still your friend. I'm still just Elbert."

He shakes his head. "Can you even call yourself human?"

The words sting, almost as much as the oar slamming against my back.

The next thing I know, my body goes topsy-turvy. Water wraps around me, sharp as the points of a lathe. The water isn't deep, so I quickly break the surface. Anne and Harold chatter downstream. They must have no idea of the pain I'm in. But I have no air in my lungs to squeeze out a cry. I lose my footing and slip under the current again. A fresh blanket of water claws my face and batters my chest. I kick my legs and comb my hands upward until my head punctures the surface.

Breathe.

It takes all I have to keep my legs kicking. Once I manage a steady pace, I'm able to scrape along the riverbed and push myself nearer to the shore. But progress is slow, and the agony overwhelms me. Meanwhile, Harold and Anne are shouting farther upriver, calling for me to wait at the riverbank. I would have laughed if I had the energy. Wait at the riverbank? My body was shooting lightning bolts of pain. I'd be lucky not to die.

A hulking creature, dark as coal and shaped like a bale of hay crashes into the water. The wolf-creature's maw, sharp as Pops's harrow, clamps onto the corner of my shirt and tugs. I don't have time to panic. I need to move. I need to *survive*.

I latch onto a patch of fur under the wolf's chin and hang on. As the creature drags me closer to the shore, streams of hot breath roll over my face. Smells like basil and peaches—Not what I expected.

My legs brush the dry sand. Gravel crunches under the bottoms of my toes until my head lands in a bed of grass. A flash of green light blinds me, and I convulse on the riverbank with my eyes squeezed shut.

A woman calls out in Spanish. Thanks to last year's Spanish language lessons, I understand some of what she says.

"M'ija, ayúdame!" Dark hair tickles my nose as one of my rescuers leans over my body.

If my Spanish is correct, she's right. I need help. I'm in pain. But even as I squint in agony, something catches my eye. The woman leaning over me has rested her hand on the ground by my nose. Her fingers press into the weeds wedged between pebbles and sand. As if sensing her touch, the plants glow green and reach for her wrist.

Magic?

I want to grab her hand and speak, but spasms of pain seize my arms and legs. Meanwhile, the sun slips down the horizon faster than the dimming of a kerosene lamp.

Or so I thought.

The sun isn't setting. I'm fainting.

Chapter Eleven

The first thing I remember is lying in a bed of fur—the wolf's back? Someone's firm grip holds me in place as wind sweeps over us. We're running through the grasses. My eyes crack open once or twice, but all I glimpse are pockets of dull, gray sky and black ribbons of hair.

A pair of arms drags me to the ground, and the heels of my feet scrape against dirt. The breeze tickling my hair goes still, and everything goes dark. I must be inside. Next thing I know, I'm lying on a flat surface. My body rolls around as my muscles spasm and twitch. My eyes are closed. I can't force them open.

Something cold prickles my skin, and several smells drift to my nose—ginger, lavender, and other earthy scents I can't name. The herbs ease the headache pounding between my eyes. Female voices whisper in Spanish, their words too swift and soft to decipher. Cool sludge tickles my skin, soothing the icy burns covering my body.

My eyes crack open, but everything is murky, like I'm staring through a dirt-smeared window. A shadow shifts to my right. My eyes flutter, focusing until I pick out an older woman's face. She pushes close, and I focus on the dent between her eyes.

Darkness swallows me up, and I'm back to that recurring dream where my body wants to fly. That same invisible force urges me off the ground, but still, my soul holds me down.

A pressure grips my fingers. Someone on the other side of this half-waking dream must be squeezing my hand. Possibly that woman from before? The sensation drags me sideways, and the dreamscape tips and fades as I climb to the waking world. Then a presence seeps into the shadows and pulls me back inside the dream—if that's what this is. I glimpse a figure with gold-green eyes, dressed in midnight. The faint outline of a shawl rings her face while the lower part of her body melts into the shadows.

"Who's there?" My voice croaks.

The figure untangles from the darkness. She's the older woman—the one with the dent in her forehead. Her piercing eyes fix on me as I slog through dust and arch for the sky. My efforts to fly, useless.

Frustration tightens my insides, then deepens into anger, and a rush of heat swirls inside of me. Soon, crackling flames spring from my hands. They pop and sizzle over the length of my back and shoulders.

The woman jumps back, her green, glowing eyes flaring. I coil my fists and draw out more flames to the backs of my arms.

The fire is part of me. It comes from me.

She grins and claps, dancing circles around my blazing body. A green haze trails in her wake. "Fénix!" her salty voice cries. Joy flows from her face.

I've heard this word before. A bird of fire that bursts from the ashes. But the way she says the word is different from the way I say "phoenix." This must be the word in Spanish.

I don't like this label she has pinned on me. It feels permanent, like I have no choice but to accept it. The light of approval brightens her eyes as I continue to burn.

"No," I say. "I'm just me. I'm normal."

The words echo, hollow and false. Even in my dreamscape, I cannot fool myself.

The old woman stops dancing and points to the west. Her shawl slips to her shoulders, and her gray-black hair flickers in the wind. I follow the direction of her hand to an orange horizon. With the help of swirling winds and slopes of brittle grass, a billowing mass of smoke stretches tall as a mountain. Fire tumbles through the fields, devouring trees, plants, buildings—and homes.

"Fénix," she whispers again.

I'm sitting in an overgrown bed of cattails. The babble of water fills my ears and sharpens my thoughts. I'm alone. But I wasn't alone before this. When did they leave me? Whoever these people are. And how did I get here?

I remember someone wedging their hands between my armpits and carrying me off somewhere. Here, apparently. I rub my eyes and shift, sensing something damp. Strips of cloth wrap my arms. My pants have been hiked above my feathery knees. I tug at the corner of a bandage. Underneath are angry welts and blistering sores—as if I'd gotten too close to a fire. A nutty herbal scent, most likely ointment for my "water burns," oozes underneath the wrappings.

When the headache pulsing behind my eyes eases to a dull ache, I remember what happened. A giant wolf pulling me to shore. A flash of green light. A woman with magic hands. And then there was the fire climbing over the hills. That must have been a dream. Right?

It takes me a little longer to hear Anne calling my name,

looking for me. Sounds like she's close to the shore. All I have to do is stand up, and we can return to the picnic together.

But that invisible cord still coils around my chest, tugging me. My body aches every second I delay.

Go back to the hills.

The urge to run digs deep into my bones. I lift my body to a crouch and hiss as the bandages tighten against my wounds. Gritting my teeth, I step toward the large indentations in the grasses—giant wolf tracks.

It isn't hard to follow the tracks of my rescuers, especially since one of them is the size of a wagon. Also, I'm pretty sure the wolf carried me to its home, fixed me up with medicines, and then hauled me back to the place it found me. That means the trail I'm following has been worn down at least two times. I follow the trail upriver past the mangroves and rope swing. Each step brings fresh bouts of pain. Soon, my body sags in exhaustion, and a seed of doubt creeps into my mind.

Maybe this is a bad idea. There's a reason they ran away before I woke up.

Then something shaped like a large pile of hay catches my eye. The object is dark and twisty, almost like a giant shrub. I crouch past bushes and trees until I'm close enough to recognize what it actually is—a shack, cobbled together with plywood and scrap metal. Ivy and grasses weave around the structure, and an unfinished porch leans toward the river. The grounds are quiet. A couple chickens, a ratty-looking goat, and the occasional dirt bunny are the only signs of life.

I blink, edging toward the hut, when a sharp crack knocks me in the head. My knees crumble, and I thud to the ground. Firecrackers burst inside my closed eyelids. I roll to face my attacker.

A girl with chocolate eyes and black rivers of hair glares down at me. She holds a shovel over her head. My mouth is numb. Can't say words yet. My head pounds in my ears.

"What are you doing here, Pollo?" she demands. She pokes me with the shovel, sending bites of pain over my water-raw skin. "Speak up, Pollo." Not a shred of patience softens her voice.

I suck in a breath. Unable to answer. To be fair, she did just whack my head with a shovel. Instead, I hold up a hand and wait for the storm in my head to pass.

"Mamá! Pollo está aquí." I don't need to know Spanish to understand her words. I'm sure she's complaining that I've come back to their home. I'm not sure why this has caused so much trouble. Didn't they just save my life?

The girl keeps the flat side of her shovel pressed to my chest.

A taller, older version of the girl appears. The woman has the same earthy skin as her daughter, same black hair, but her eyes are different. True, they are a warm brown like her daughter's, but at certain angles, a flash of green rings the iris.

"M'ija, que pasó?" Mother and daughter exchange more words of Spanish. My ears strain to catch their words—not that I know much Spanish. But there's an urgency to their voices. A panic.

The girl points to me. "I don't know why he's here, Máma," she says in English.

With the girl's eyes averted, I dare to nudge the shovel an inch sideways. My reward is a sharp pinch as the girl presses down harder. This brings a fresh burst of pain, and the mother yanks the shovel out of her daughter's hands. I'm grateful for this, but I'm not sure if I have the strength to stand alone. I hope one of them offers me a hand, and soon. Bugs are crawling up my legs.

An older woman shuffles to the scene. She stares me down with the same vibrant green eyes as the first woman. I squint at her face and recognize her gray-streaked hair and the dent between her eyes.

This is the woman from my dream.

She cracks a smile and says something in Spanish. Her voice is weighed down with age, and I can't understand a thing she says. She seems old enough to be the girl's grandmother.

Mother and Daughter ignore Grandmother and continue arguing about something—me, probably. Grandmother peers down at me.

"Pollo no comprende el español, Abuelita," the girl says to Grandmother.

It's true. I don't speak Spanish. Barely understand the easy words.

Grandmother glances at the squabbling women and offers me a calloused hand. She yanks me upright and pats me on the back.

"Hola," I croak and clench my muscles, failing to hide my shivering limbs. The grandmother leans toward me. She smells like mint and cinnamon.

"Hola, m'ijo. Hablas español?" She has the same gritty voice as the woman in my dream. She wants to know if I understand Spanish, but I can't recall any words except—

"Hola," I repeat, quietly this time. "Ah, soy Elbert."

She crosses her arms and blinks at me. Then she laughs, rich and earthy.

Mother and Daughter halt their conversation to stare at us.

"Abuelita?" The girl reaches for Grandmother, who continues laughing.

Grandmother bats the girl away and reaches for my hand instead. "My name, Flor." She points to the other woman and says, "This, my daughter, Lupe Padilla."

"Hola," I say and lift a hand in greeting.

Grandmother glances at the frowning girl with taut eyebrows and tumbling black hair.

"Valora," she mumbles as an afterthought.

Chapter Twelve

My head grazes low-hanging herbs as I step into the three women's hut. Vials of spices and medicines crowd bookshelves and cabinets. A peppery scent tickles my nose, and a whiff of something sharp and sweet reminds me of spiced apples. A partially dyed garment drapes over the side of a bucket in the corner. To my right, neatly positioned on a shallow stool, a stone figurine of a woman clasps her hands with her head bent to the side. A blue shawl with yellow stars drapes down from her head to her ankles. The way she's leaning forward with her head tilted like that reminds me of the Virgin Mary.

"Why are you here?" Valora speaks fiercely as a wolf. Lupe Padilla stands over her daughter, curiosity flashing green in her eyes.

Now that I have their full attention, my words crumble to dust.

Valora's face softens slightly. "Can't you speak?" She seems genuinely concerned about me. More likely, she thinks I'm a simpleton.

"Thank you for saving me, Valora," I croak. "Thank you,

Mrs. Padilla." I glance at Grandmother and add, "Gracias, Señora Flor."

She smiles and taps my arm. She points to herself and says, "Abuelita."

She wants me to call her "Grandma" in Spanish? This is an honor. A jealous scoff from Valora confirms this.

Abuelita ignores her granddaughter and motions me to take a seat at their small wooden table. If you could call it that. A jagged top layer of pine has been attached to iron rods. Twisting vines tangle the wood and iron together, making the table sturdier than I expected. In the center is a wooden bowl full of peaches. This makes me grin.

Hmm. Where did they get these?

Abuelita grabs my hand like she already knows me. She was there in my dream, but did she *live* the dream with me? It's hard to keep up with all these strange happenings. Her grip tightens like she's claiming me as her friend. Like she knows me. Maybe she does. Maybe these people can help me understand who I am.

"M'ijo," says Mrs. Padilla. "Why did you come here?"

"I'm here because..." I pause. At this point, the rope around my chest, the one that pulled me to these women, snaps. A pressure builds behind my eyes as the questions I've longed to ask can finally be voiced.

No. Please don't cry in front of these women.

I blink back my feelings and say, "I want to know if I'm like you."

I study all their faces and try to identify which one is the wolf—maybe all three. I have no way of knowing because right now, they all look human. They look *normal*. But they've found a way to hide the wild parts of themselves—unlike me.

"I want to know something first," Valora says, pointing to the feathers poking through the collar of my shirt. "What's wrong with your magic?"

"I'm sorry, Elbert," Mrs. Padilla says, throwing Valora a glare and pulling her daughter to the side. She whispers a short sentence in Spanish. Valora cocks her head at me before spitting another sentence back at her mom. It sounds surly, but I don't understand the words. She could have been discussing the weather for all I knew. Mrs. Padilla nudges Valora away from the table, and the girl sulks to a different corner of the room.

"Now. About your question. Are we the same?" Mrs. Padilla and Abuelita exchange glances. Mrs. Padilla seats herself and starts inspecting me. She prods my arms and feet and gingerly traces the feathers growing near the backs of my ears. "It looks—half-finished."

"What? Half-finished?"

"Like a half-finished spell." She shakes her head. "This is not the same as us."

I've got a half-finished curse? How's that possible?

"Can I get rid of it?" I ask. This *could* be good news. Something half-done might mean it can be undone.

Mrs. Padilla glances over to the window. The sun has slipped under the hills, and the sky is sinking into a grayish-blue. "Come back tomorrow, m'ijo. The day is late."

Valora huffs behind me. "Ay dios, Mamá! You told him to come *back*?"

"Please—uh—Por favor." I plead, peering up at Mrs. Padilla's stern face. "Once I go back home, Mom and Pops will ground me for leaving the church picnic. I won't be able to come again."

"Then don't go home, Pollo." I can hear the eye roll in Valora's voice. "Go back down the river. Let them find you there."

Not a bad idea.

"His name is Elbert, m'ija. Don't call him 'Pollo' anymore." Mrs. Padilla winces in my direction. "Sorry, Elbert.

Sometimes we make names for people around town. Yours was easy because, well, pollo means chicken, and you're—a bird. Kind of. We noticed your feathers."

"It's okay," I say. "I don't mind nicknames."

A husky laugh escapes Abuelita's lips. She has caught on to the nature of our discussion. Possibly.

Mrs. Padilla offers to help me to my feet. "Tomorrow, m'ijo."

"Okay," I agree. "But can I come during midday break? I have chores every morning and sometimes in the evening."

Abuelita tugs my arm. "Yes, come." Her eagerness to see me hits my heart just right, and her effort to speak English makes her words earnest and close. Like a friend.

"Gracias." I wish I could say more than a simple "thank you," but it's more than enough. Abuelita's eyes are melting. I don't know what I've done to earn such acceptance.

I nod and stumble out of the opening. I want to hide the mist collecting in my eyes.

"Wait!" Valora jogs over to me. The scowl on her face wavers when she comes. "Are you okay, Pollo?" Her eyes are wide, concerned.

I ignore the way my heart flips sideways as her eyes dig into mine, and I force myself to consider her question. Even though Mrs. Padilla says I'm not like them, she has welcomed me. Because of this, something warm is unfurling in my chest.

"I'm great, Valora." It's the first time I say her name, and her step stutters. But only briefly. She continues light-footed through the thorny brush and bristles. I stride alongside her until she stops.

"Wait," she says, pinching my forearm.

I screech to a halt. My skin tingles under the weight of her fingers. She peers into my face, and my cheeks tingle, probably turning red. Then, as if finding what she was looking for, she relaxes. "Follow me."

I hope this means I passed her test. It appears she trusts me enough to show me the way home. Not that I need her help. But I won't be complaining, either.

We retrace our steps through the open grasses until we near a grove of trees by the river. Her brow wrinkles, and she studies my eyes until I look away. "I haven't gotten mine yet," she says wistfully.

"Gotten what?"

She shrugs like she doesn't care, but then she sighs. Only a person who cares would sigh like that. "Magic," she says. "I can't change shape yet."

Her confession knocks me off-balance. Did I hear that right? Does she *want* to be cursed?

"Mamá says soon." Valora continues. "She says she'll help me grow my spark into magic I can control. Possibly when I turn fourteen."

Her words rustle up a sourness in my gut. Is that what happened to me? I somehow got a *spark* of magic? But still, it's growing. Without my permission.

"When did your spark start growing? When you turned thirteen?" she says.

"Not until after I turned fourteen," I say.

She quiets as we near the riverbank. "I've never known another person, other than my family, to have a spark before. I can't imagine growing my spark alone."

My face must be serious because Valora pats my shoulder and cracks a smile. Her eyes are still sharp, even with a smile tugging at her lips. "Well, you aren't alone anymore. You have us now, El—" She hesitates. "What's your name again?"

"Elbert. That's my name."

"*El Bert?*" She speaks my name like two words. I try to

swallow my smile, but I must have failed because she scowls. "What's so funny?"

"*El*bert," I say again, emphasizing the *El* in my name.

"Ahh," she nods. "Okay. Goodbye, Elberto. Ah! *El*bert." She squinches her face.

"Thank you," I say.

A flush blossoms on her cheeks. "But really, Elbert. I'm sorry. I wasn't nice to you before."

I nod. It's true.

"And I hit you..." she points to my head, "... with a shovel."

I shrug. "It's okay."

"Ay! No, it's not, Elbert. Are you crazy?" She smiles and breathes in as if preparing to laugh. Then, just as suddenly, her eyes darken. "I need to protect them, you know." Her mouth clenches. "If you hurt Abuelita or Máma, I will hurt you back."

It's a promise. Even though it's directed at me, I feel a deep sense of respect for this girl. I'm not worried. I have no plans to hurt these women.

"Okay," I agree. We've now reached the river. The rest of the way is clear, and as I sense Valora preparing to leave, I remember the strawberries growing in our home garden. Is it possible?

"Wait! I know you've been stealing from the orchard, but did you plant a strawberry patch in our garden?"

Without a hint of guilt, she cocks an eyebrow and tips her head to the side. "I have no idea what you're talking about."

Chapter Thirteen

Before I trudge along the riverbed, I take off my bandages and wipe the ointment off my skin. Voices in the distance call out my name, so I follow until Finn scrambles along the riverbank and latches onto my arm. He flags down Mom and Pops. Apparently, they were just beyond the thicket. After helping me back to the main group, Mom and Pops want to take me home immediately.

"You could have drowned, Elby. You need to get home. Maybe call Dr. Brownly in the morning," Mom says.

"I'm fine, Mom. And I didn't drown." I keep quiet about the water burns. I don't want her worrying about my raw skin. Not to mention the feathers sprouting all over my body.

"We'll at least call Dr. Brownly tomorrow, just in case," she says.

I don't fight her. She's being extra careful, just like she's careful with all of us.

Trinna bounces over to me and gently links arms. She makes lofty promises about gathering me food, but I know better than to hope.

"Okay," Mom relents. "You can stay." Trinna squeals and chases down the nearest cob of corn.

Soon after that, Anne finds me and nearly falls at my feet with apologies. I remind her that I agreed to do the race. I knew the dangers. That seems to ease her guilt. Meanwhile, Harold is nowhere to be seen. I hope it's because he feels guilty for nearly sending me to my death.

"Just so you know, I won the race," Anne brags as she sticks a stray foxtail between her teeth. "And *you* lost."

I should grin or laugh or say something funny, but my heart is too heavy for that.

We spend the rest of the evening huddling around a bonfire, munching on Trinna's stash of food. This includes bread with lemon butter, blackberry pie—what's left of it—and sticky globs of taffy wrapped in wax paper.

At some point, Anne widens her eyes.

"What is it?" I ask, swiping my face for stray crumbs.

"Oh, it's just. I didn't notice it before, but..." She points at my face. "The firelight makes your eyes glow reddish gold."

That's surprising. No one has mentioned this before, and I haven't seen my face reflected in anything recently but a spoon. It reminds me of the glowing green-eyed women in the woods. More evidence proving I am like them.

I'm just glad Anne doesn't think glowing eyes are strange.

"Thank you," I mumble and sink back into my thoughts.

I have so many questions boiling inside of me and no one who can listen, so, for my peace of mind, I let my thoughts wander as I watch the people around me. A group of children whirl their child-sized American flags, and I smile at old couples swaying to the rhythm of a peppy tune, courtesy of the accordion man. Soon, a woman leans next to him with a fiddle. Her nimble fingers dance as she bounces her bow against the strings. Mom and Pops join in with the other dancers. Pops catches me staring and winks back, tugging Mom closer to his chest.

Some of the younger children wag their toy guns while others bounce past with their toy cannons loaded with blank cartridges. One girl with a ratty ponytail sneaks up to unsuspecting adults and fires her cannon over their heads. Then she channels the ghosts of Civil War past by crying out, "For freedom!"

Just beyond the crowd, I catch a glimpse of Vida and Daichi walking along the riverbed. Their hands are clasped together while Daichi's jacket rests on Vida's shoulders.

When the last breath of sunlight sinks below the horizon, a handful of men move to the riverbed. They choose a shallow spot on the water and set up a wooden table. Soon, firecrackers sputter and zip into the night sky. We shriek and holler as they blot out the stars with flashes of light. This goes on for a while, and my mind wanders. I remember the roaring fire from my dreams, and deep down, a pit forms. Is something dangerous burning its way to us? I don't know what it could be, but I can already smell its bitter scent in the air and the heat rising from the dirt.

"Elbert!" Anne's voice calls in the back of a dream. My eyes fling open.

Did I doze off?

She's already on her feet and yanking my arm. "Didn't you hear me? There's a fire!"

"Fire? How? When?" Guilt sweeps over me. Did I start a fire?

"One of the fireworks landed on a tree."

A mass of bodies rush past me—small ones, large ones, young ones, old and slow-moving ones. All of them are running from a sharp, crackling mass of orange light.

I recognize Leo. "Get going, boy!" he calls as he hobbles past.

A rush of energy snaps me into focus, and I spring to my feet. Is this magic shooting up and down my body?

"What are you doing?" Anne shouts with a rasp in her voice.

I don't know what to say. My instinct would normally be to run to safety. But my bones pull me to the flames as the heat draws me in. My feet inch forward even as the flames latch onto the next tree, then onto the nearest patch of grass. I grip the trunk of a smoldering tree, dig my heels into the ground, lean forward, and push.

Chapter Fourteen

The tree doesn't budge, not at first, but the sizzling heat springs over my shoulders and adds to my strength.

I push again.

Curled roots rip free of the earth as the blackened trunk leans under the force of my arms. The trunk sways and considers breaking.

A handful of voices snag my attention. Several men and women are lugging buckets back and forth from the river and tossing water across the glowing mounds of shrubs and grasses. I recognize Peto as one of them. And there's Daichi helping two or three other men dunk one of the paddle boats into the river until it sinks, then four or five more join to lift it from the water.

I turn back to the blistering trunk, grit my teeth, and push again. It won't move.

"Mama!" A quivering voice breaks my concentration. It's coming from a patch of sizzling grass.

I leave the stubborn tree and rush to the voice. I find the girl with the ratty ponytail crying in the folds of a bush. She's clutching her toy cannon as flames creep toward her. I stretch

84

my arms into the burning grasses and pull her free, then hoist her onto my back. She doesn't complain about my feathers or my overly hot skin. She just holds on.

I run. The sores on my legs chafe in my pants as I veer into the breeze, and the weight of the girl irritates the welts on my arms, but I bite my lip and push my way through the dark. I arrive at a crowd of people standing a safe distance from the lake.

"Mama!" The girl squirms out of my arms and tumbles to the ground.

I return to the fire.

I find three more people. One is an older man with a missing arm, a veteran from the Civil War. I crash through the flames rolling in on all sides and lift him with strength I never knew I had. I grab two more children, one as young as three. I don't wait for their thanks. I just drop them to safety and rush back to the fire.

When I go back for another round, I glimpse a man moving between the smoke and flames.

There's a man who can touch fire without flinching? Who is this?

I follow him as he heads toward the bodies of fire devouring the trees by the waterside. When I reach a patch of smoldering bushes, I lose sight of him. By now, the flames have spread to areas beyond the reach of the men and women throwing pails of water and wet blankets. They're driving a line of water upriver, but downriver, the flames are eating their way toward the nearest field of sugar beets.

I lean back, searching for ideas to stop this fire when something rustles in the corner of my eye.

A tendril of fire unlatches from a smoldering tree and reaches toward *me*.

An unmanly screech jumps from my mouth.

What is *this*?

The arm of fire ducks backward. Does it sense my fear? How strange! I move to my right, and so does the fiery tendril. I move left, and the tendril swerves with me. Soon, more tendrils join the first one. I jerk my arm above my head, and the orange flames shoot higher than the tree limbs. Then they arch over to me until they swirl between my fingers.

Woah! Am I *controlling* this fire?

I fling my hand toward the meandering river. The fire jumps, like a dog chasing a branch, stopping just shy of the stream. As I move with the fire, bursts of energy rumble through my body. It's thrilling, the tingling power of fire, but it's also exhausting.

I better move fast.

I claw my arms through the air as I struggle to the water, hoping the movements will attract as many flames as possible. Then, once I'm inches from the stream, I twist around, keeping my arms taut and wide.

A blanket of rippling fire spreads toward me, angling for my hands. The crackling roar reminds me of churning river rapids—harsh, brutal, and unrelenting. I clench my fists as my grip on the flames starts to slip. Gusts of wind whip against the embers, coaxing the fire further down the river. I yank my hold on the flames toward the water, but there's resistance, like pulling the reins of a stubborn horse. The strain on my already battered body nearly brings me to my knees. My bones ache, and a metallic taste seeps into my mouth.

Someone is calling my name. I don't know who. But it doesn't matter. I can't concentrate on two things right now.

I swivel in the mud, take a deep breath, and slam my hand into the water. Golden ropes of fire twist and crash against the Upside Down River. I scream as the water rubs against my raw hands. Rising vapors confirm the fire's time of death.

I push myself harder, but my grip on the flames slips like I've exhausted my magic. A piercing pain snaps through my head, followed by a throbbing ache. My body twists in agony, but I can't stop. I have to pull this fire to the river.

Someone calls out behind me. "I found him!" It's a husky voice. Young. Familiar.

Valora came back?

The distraction throws me off-balance, and I lose my grip on a handful of flames. The flames slide along the dirt until they find a shrub to chew on. My legs melt to jelly, and I dip to the ground. A set of hands, large and firm, pulls me back to my feet.

Not Valora's hands. Had I imagined her?

"Breathe, Son." It's Pops. "Try to relax. Focus." He presses both hands against my back.

I take a deep breath and exhale, and the hammering in my head starts to relax. A few more breaths ease out of my lungs. My gaze lands on Pops first. His face is smeared with soot. Behind his shoulder is *not* Valora, but Anne. She's holding an empty bucket in her hands.

"He's okay," she announces, more to herself. Then she digs her bucket into the water and hurries to fight the flames.

Pops waits for her to disappear behind the folds of trees. When he glances back at me, I notice something I had not noticed before. A golden ring burning in his eyes.

"Pops?" My voice is barely above a whisper. "What's in your eyes?"

If he heard me, he doesn't respond. Instead, he steps away, raises his arm, and points to the flames spilling down the river-bank. The flames slither through the grasses, unwrap from the trees, and coil around his shoulders. They twist into a fiery wheel and hover above his arm. The wheel of fire grows as more flames disentangle from the brambles and latch onto him.

Anger builds behind my eyes as my father works a magic

he has been hiding from the world. He draws the fire with his head down, as if ashamed. It all feels so—forbidden.

"You never told me!" I shout. I didn't plan to say these words out loud, not while he was manipulating the flames. But I'm sick with anger.

Pops pauses in his fire wrangling long enough to say, "Don't move, Son! You've overdone it already."

He reaches out, reeling in tongues of flames. Just when the wheel of fire twisting around his arm looks like it will spin out of control, he dunks his arm into the river. Vapors rise like spirits, and a gust of warm wind hurries in to sweep aside the haze.

Anne returns, skidding past a smoking bush. "Elbert, did you do that?" She pushes her speckled nose close to my face. "I saw this huge fire. So, I ran over."

"No," I say. "It was…" I point to where Pops should be. But he's not there.

"That was amazing," she shakes her head. "Amazing! We stopped the fire. Can you believe it? How did you water everything so fast? I can't believe you did that alone."

I know I should be proud in this moment. I helped stop a large portion of the fire from growing into a beast beyond our control. But Pops was the one who saved the day. Normally, I would be proud of Pops for what he did. But I'm not proud of him. I'm—it's hard to explain. There's this hollowness in my gut. A sickness.

"Have you seen my pops?"

As I say the words, Pops rounds the bend. He's holding a pail of water, blinking at us with a bewildered expression. Like he's an average citizen and not a man who has just performed great magic.

"Mr. Dowden, did you see Elbert stop the fire?" says Anne. She tugs my father over to me, oblivious to the fact Pops is actually the one who saved us all.

"Can I chat with my pops alone, please?" I ask.

She sighs and leans in to hug me. I'm afraid to touch her, afraid I might burn her, but she doesn't flinch.

"Thank you," she murmurs and leaves.

Pops stares at me silently. All traces of fiery gold are gone from his eyes.

A storm of thoughts rumbles through me. Pops is cursed. And I'm cursed because he's cursed, just like the Padilla family. They pass down a magic spark from one generation to the next. From mother to daughter. From father to son.

"Why didn't you tell me?" My voice breaks.

Pops gave this spark to me. But how? When? Why didn't he warn me about this? And why don't Vida and Peto have this?

Tears burn my cheeks. I don't try to stop them. I can't stop them. All this time. I've felt so alone, so *wrong*, abandoned in silence—this is the poison of secrets. Pops knew I might be struggling with this, could have warned me, yet he chose to be silent.

Pops slouches his eyebrows, and his eyes dim. He opens his mouth. Nothing comes out. I'm digging out the truth from him, and all he does is crumble to pieces.

"Admit it." A snarl strangles my words.

Fear paralyzes his body the way it paralyzed me when I stared at Mr. Halifax in the Riverside Hotel. I don't like his timid response, and I don't like remembering this weakness in me. Fat tears roll down his cheeks and catch the ends of his mustache. I search for the gold spark in his eyes. All I find is an old sadness, a look I've seen many times.

"You're ashamed of me." I speak the words like an accusation.

The words hit like flint against stone. And there it is, the orange spark—just a flash. It illuminates his eyes, and then it's gone.

"No, Son. I'm not ashamed of you. Not at all," Pops finally says. His shoulders sink, like a weight is pressing on his soul. This weight passes onto me, a numbing burden that pools in the bottom of my gut.

I clench my fists. "Well?" That can't be all he has to say. He's been hiding the truth from me this entire time. He's been letting me believe a *lie*.

"I'm sorry, Son. I should have told you." His voice is hoarse. "But telling you—it would only make your spark grow. You said you wanted to be ordinary, but for this to happen, you must ignore that spark. Let it snuff out. That's what Vida did, and that's what Peto did. They both wanted ordinary lives, so I ignored the spark inside them. I let them choose that ordinary choice. Telling them would have made it so much harder to ignore that spark. The same goes for you."

I rub my forehead, trying to piece this information together. "It kept building inside me. I couldn't just ignore it."

His eyes lower like he's about to say some very bad news. "That means deep down, whether you know it or not, you want more than just an ordinary life."

Does he really think I *want* this curse? I've been doing everything I can to hide these changes. If I could simply ignore this and make it disappear, I would have done that.

"How do I get rid of it?"

He hesitates. I force myself not to grab his shoulders and shake the words from his mouth.

"Pops," anger deepens my voice, "how do I get rid of this curse?"

"I don't know. But if that's what you want, I will find a cure." He says this with certainty, or maybe it's fierce desperation.

A cure? There's a cure? "Is that possible?"

"Let me worry about this," he says. "The more you know

about your curse, the harder it will be to stomp out. I have to search alone."

There is hope in the way he speaks. It's not a warm, joyful hope. It's more like an enduring loyalty to this promise he's made. Then his face darkens. "Don't let anyone know I stopped the fire."

My mouth pops open. He wants me to *lie*? "Why?"

"Because," he says and faces Mom, who is sliding down the embankment, "I'm hiding, too."

When she reaches us, she clutches me to her side. Vida and Peto are with her, and they help drag my wobbly legs across the field to the wagon. I ease into the back with Trinna and Jorm. Resentment gnaws on my gut as Pops leaves without saying a word, joining Peto on the bikes.

As the wagon cuts a path through the field, I rest my head on a bed of blankets and stare at the blackened sky. Tonight, the moon is thin and quiet, nearly swallowed by a shadow.

Chapter Fifteen

I slip into an older time—and place. We're working the farm, and Pops is still learning how to cultivate sugar beets. Everything is crisp. The rich earth crumbles under my hands and a hot gust of air sprays from Fuzzy Lips' nostrils. I smell the comforting scent of wet grass. The blue hills sleep in the distance under a sky smeared with clouds.

We're in the rainy season when the sky dribbles on our backs. A few hired fieldhands work the seedbeds with Pops, who grimaces under the harsh labor. But it's not just the work that causes pain. His rain-soaked skin is red like he's been out in the sun for too long.

Everything shifts and more familiar moments rustle to life.

Pops sits by the hearth, staring at the dark clouds looming on the horizon. Peto and I dare each other to run outside during the downpour. When we slosh into the house, soaked and shivering, Mom throws wool blankets at us and orders us to pile our sopping clothes in a bucket. Pops sits in the corner, his ashen face staring at nothing as he refuses to walk outside, even after the clouds have pushed their way past the hills.

"Your Pops has got weak lungs." Mom's voice flickers in the corner, somewhere in the inky shadows.

That's not true. Pops is strong. He can lift lumber large enough to build a house. There must be some other reason. But I can't remember. Not right now.

More familiar moments bleed into the scene—Peto and I running outside to fix the horse pen or to chase down Howly when the thunder blares too close. We rush back to Pops who bows over the fire, not a drop of rain ever touching his head.

I remember Peto explaining that "Pops is ashamed of his weakness."

His weakness. This phrase burns in my mind. I should know this. This means something.

But I'm lost to the whims of these old memories because now Pops's silhouette leans against the glare of firelight. A deep, aching sadness presses against my back and seeps into my chest. It numbs my muscles and reassures me that I ought to stay put.

Don't move. Stay.

I lie flat on the ground next to Pops, who sags in his chair. We slump like this in my dream of memories—for what feels like a very long time.

The next morning, a pudgy little hand latches onto my big toe. However, instead of the usual wiggling and giggling, I'm greeted with an ear-splitting scream.

I lurch forward in my bed and face Finn's brown eyes peering back at me in horror.

"Elby!" he shrieks. "What happened to your feet?"

I shake off the bedsheet and reveal long, spindly toes with sharp nails poking out the ends. What is this? These look like bird feet!

I scream. Loudly. Top of my lungs. "Woah! I don't know."

Now I really look like a chicken. How far is this curse going to transform me?

Jorm runs into the room, takes a good look at me, and gasps, nearly falling to the floor. "Elbert! Why's your hair so red? And what happened to your face?"

Oh, no. There's more on my face?

I trace my fingers along my cheek and neck. A fresh patch of feathers is now climbing from my chest up to my face. It's like Pops said—the more I know about this curse, the more I lose control of this spark. I've doubled my growth of feathers in one night.

The door whips open, and Pops strides into the room. Peto hovers in the doorway, and Vida peeks around his shoulder. Everyone squawks and screams. Little Finn cries. Then Pops takes everyone aside to tell them the things I already know. I've got this magic spark inside me. I can't seem to stop it from growing. Now, all I can do is wait for a cure. If there is one.

It takes a few days for everyone to adjust to my new condition. Finn accepts me first, just like he accepts our ghostly sister. It's in his nature, so of course he'll be the first to see past the feathers. Peto and Vida just feel sorry for me, mostly because they managed to escape this curse. I wasn't as lucky as them. Trinna is fascinated by me, asking questions at every turn, tagging along everywhere I go. Mom already knew about this strange family trait, but seeing it passed onto me brings her a sadness, like she's watching me slowly die.

A couple of days after my family found out who I *really* am, Anne shows up on our front porch. She balances a basket on one arm and asks to see me, mostly to make sure I'm feeling okay after stopping a forest fire. I hope she hasn't come to ask questions because I haven't prepared any answers. Harold was always the one with answers to things we didn't want to talk about.

She screams when she sees me. No surprise there. I try to explain my situation, tell her I'm still Elbert, just working out this magic that's slowly swallowing me whole. Finally, she calms down long enough to sit with me and share her sourdough bread and berry tarts. I try to have a normal conversation with her—talk about my plans for the fall, the upcoming harvest, things like that. Her gaze is either lost somewhere else or fixed on my feathery face. By the end of her visit, she has learned not to stare, and I believe she is trying to accept me for who I am. When she leaves, I don't expect her to return.

Word circles through town. A few townsfolk find an excuse to stop by the farm. I always keep my distance as they chat with Pops. I don't feel like being observed right now.

Leo drops by at some point to unload an order for Pops. The grizzled blacksmith takes one glance at me and says, "Lookin' fluffy, Elby." That's all he says. His eyes don't inspect the feathers on my face, his mouth doesn't crinkle into a frown, and he doesn't give a sideways glare as he walks to his horse-drawn cart. Instead, he tosses a wave and a smile. "Be sure to fly on by the shop sometime."

I don't mind that he's poking fun. Most people say nothing while their fearful eyes do all the talking. Meanwhile, I've stopped speaking to Pops. He may share this curse with me, and he may be the only person who understands what I'm going through, but his dishonesty doesn't sit right. I don't remember Pops ever lying before.

It's strange, not speaking to a person I've known my whole life. I still acknowledge him, saying things like "hello" and "good night," but I haven't looked him in the eyes. Not since they turned orange-gold. Besides, the more he talks to me about this curse, the more I'll turn into this hideous creature.

At least, that's what *he* thinks. Lately, I haven't been so sure. I've done everything I can to ignore what's happening to my body, all the sudden changes, and I've pushed away all my frustrations and irritations with Pops and the curse. Still, every morning, a fresh patch of feathers appears. At this rate, I'll be growing wings.

Oh, no. What if I grow a beak?

It takes a couple more days for me to realize this, but eventually, it hits me. Ignoring the curse is not working. If I'm going to stop this curse, I have to face it straight on, and I have to talk to someone about it.

It's time to speak to the shapeshifters by the river.

Chapter Sixteen

Today, I finish my chores before the midday lull approaches. Then I grab a bike and cut a path through the brush alongside the Upside Down River. Anxiety pinches my side as I close the distance between the Padillas' home and myself. I'm worried the answers won't be what I want to hear. I'm worried I'll lose any last bit of control I have over this magic. But it's worth finding out.

I've developed a new fear—never undoing the curse. So far, these women have embraced their abilities, even if it means hiding in a small, makeshift home in the middle of nowhere.

Still seems like a curse to me.

I jump off my bike and wheel my way to the small clearing. I don't want to surprise these women. Not like last time. I scan my surroundings and notice a smoldering pile of trash nearly burnt to cinders. Someone was here recently.

A sharp movement catches the corner of my eye. It's coming from the river, so I lean my bike against a thicket and pick my way through the knee-high weeds until I'm standing just shy of the water. Piled on a bed of grass is a brightly patterned shawl, and a few feet from that is a shovel. Valora's weapon of choice.

I rub the sore spot on my head and smile. It was kind of funny. I got hit in the head *twice* that day. First by Harold with his oar, and then by a girl living in the hills surrounded by shapeshifting beasts.

Life is odd.

To my left, beyond the weeds, a splash wrinkles the water, and a crocodile the size of a fisherman's boat floats into view. The mid-summer stream is shallow, so the beast brushes its legs against the river bottom. Lounging on top of the giant reptile is Valora wearing a red dress. The sun glows orange on her back as she tucks her arms under her chin and kicks her legs up and down. She shifts her gaze, most likely noting my recent developments—overgrown toes, burnt-red hair—but she says nothing.

I should be shocked. Terrified. A giant creature is floating in the Upside Down River with a girl clinging to its back. But after what I've seen these past few days...

I remember the news articles from Mr. Halifax's room about the other creatures—the stag, the wolf, and the crocodile. I have met the stag and the wolf, but now, here before me, is the crocodile. A shapeshifting crocodile?

"Mrs. Padilla? Is that you?" My body tingles, almost like it's warning me there's danger ahead. It reminds me of the time I saw the wolf in the garden a few nights ago.

"She's not Mamá." Valora yawns. She digs her fingers into the meandering stream and grabs a stick floating in the water. She uses the jagged edge to scratch the crocodile's back. A satisfying sound churns the water by the creature's jaws.

The crocodile angles its head in my direction and starts floating toward me. The feathers on the back of my neck prickle as the creature creeps closer. Its lidless eyes glow green.

Just then, a disturbance rumbles the damp earth. Something large is thudding against the brush.

A mountain of dark gray fur halts just an arm's length away. The massive head of a wolf with glowing green eyes peers down at me. It wrinkles its snout and breathes hot air onto my face. The sight of the beast steals my breath away, and I jump back. My nerves prickle like static. Or is that magic rustling to life? A spark spins in my gut. The last time I saw this beast, I was barely conscious. Now, in the midday light, it's obvious how intimidating this creature really can be.

"Hola, Mamá. How'd your search go?" Valora says behind me. She lands barefoot on the bank of the river and crunches through the brittle weeds, heading for the towering wolf. She sinks into the creature's chest, losing her arms in a bed of fur.

Valora's interruption breaks the tension building in my body, and I breathe normally again.

So Mrs. Padilla is the wolf? I suppose that means the crocodile is—

"Abuelita?" I say before I turn to face her.

A blinding green light pokes my eyes. As the light flickers and dies, it leaves behind a cloud of green, glittering dust. The dust meanders toward us, and a tart scent pinches my nose and burns its way to the back of my eyes. Soon, my head fills with sand.

A fresh wave of panic grips me, and I forget that the wolf in front of me is my ally. At this moment, she's a monster. I open my mouth to scream, but no sound comes out. I can't hear anything above the shrieking winds. I can't see past the shadow covering my eyes.

Wait. I remember this wind and the way it swirls and sucks away voices. I remember it from the day the stag disappeared —how it confused my senses and tricked my thoughts.

I cough as more dust burns my nose, and my thoughts bend again.

Wait. What's happening? I sense the towering presence darkening the sky in front of me. Should I be worried about this giant beast? Should I attack it before it attacks me? Heat rushes through my blood and gathers at the palms of my hands. My shoulders burn. What's that? Someone is calling my name, and a pair of hands grip my face. How long have those been there? I reach up and touch them. These are small hands. Rough and calloused. Like they've been digging trenches in the dirt with—a shovel.

Valora?

My vision clears. Was it blurry before?

The pressure of Valora's hands pulls me back from the frayed edges of my mind. At the same time, the swirling winds lose momentum and die. I meet Valora's dark eyes and realize what she's doing. She's holding me while I'm on the verge of bursting into flames. Afraid I might burn her, I wrench her arms away, realizing too late that my hands are crackling with fire.

She yelps and jumps backward.

"Valora!" I yell.

She sits in the dirt and cradles her arms. Then I glance at the wolf and remember. This is not a creature waiting to tear me to pieces. This is Lupe Padilla. And that bright green flash? That was a crocodile shifting into a human.

My head throbs as my mind continues to untangle itself.

"Are you okay?" Valora gingerly reaches for my shoulder, and I notice finger-shaped blisters on her skin. A deep part of me wants to scoop her up and hold her, but I can't. I'll only hurt her again.

Won't I?

"I'm so sorry," I say, my stomach twisting.

She shakes her head. "Mamá will just make an ointment... like the one she made for you. It's fine. I'll be fine."

This puts me more at ease, but I still feel sick to my stomach.

Abuelita is in human form now and shuffling toward me with sopping wet hair. She hugs her shawl to her shoulders and offers a shivering smile. The only evidence that she was lazing around as a crocodile is the slimy grass tangled in her hair and the gritty, river-water scent on her skin. She reaches for my hand and squeezes, grinning and patting me on the back.

"Buenos dias, m'ijo."

Chapter Seventeen

Mrs. Padilla was kind enough to shift back to human form at a distance behind their makeshift home. The same cloud of dust balloons into the area, but by the time it reaches me, it has faded to a low haze. The tangy scent that would twist my mind never reaches my nose.

As if to apologize for casting a spell on me, Abuelita prepares a meal of hand-kneaded tortillas and fixings. She uses a makeshift stove that's basically a milking pail flipped upside down. Several holes gouged along the sides act as vents.

"Can you light this, Elbert?" Mrs. Padilla nudges a handful of brambles and two blocks of wood through an opening at the base of the pail.

I peer at the kindling and hold back an anxious sigh. Controlling fire is one thing. Pulling fire from my gut until it crackles in my hand—I'm still getting the hang of that. I concentrate until heat pools in my right hand. I rub my fingers together, and a spark lights the base of my palm. Soon, curls of fire weave between my fingers.

That was easy. I must be getting better at this.

I think back on the river fire only a couple of days ago. I

remember how the flames had curled toward me, eager to obey the wave of my hand. And Pops, how he balanced a swirl of fire around his forearm. He had been so confident, as if he were simply tugging sacks of grain off the wagon. I remember how the flames swirled over him, bending at the flick of his wrist. Then I think of Harold, the fear in his eyes, the spark lighting up his shirt.

The fire in my hand sputters out.

"You okay, Elbert?" Mrs. Padilla says.

I focus on my hand again, this time clenching my nails against the skin of my palm until another spark lights my fingers. I flick a tuft of fire onto the tinder. Once the fire shows steady signs of life, Abuelita slides an iron pan over the top of the upside-down pail. Soon, her sausage links and tomatoes sputter in the pan. She mixes ground chili peppers and cracks a few eggs. As the eggs form solid lumps, she sprinkles in cilantro and salt.

We sit cross-legged on patches of grass and eat from ceramic bowls, except for Mrs. Padilla, who eats directly from the pan. I suppose they don't usually entertain guests. Never needed an extra bowl until now.

I follow Valora's movements as she tears strips of her tortilla and uses them to scoop out lumps of egg and sausage. I take a bite and pause to let the flavors fill my mouth. The simple ingredients comfort me like a childhood memory.

"Do you like it?" Mrs. Padilla watches me take a bite. A shade of uncertainty lingers in her voice.

"It's perfect," I say without hesitation.

She tells Abuelita, who lets out a rusty laugh followed by a few words in Spanish.

Valora smirks and digs another strip of tortilla into her bowl. "Abuelita says it's not true Mexican style. But we use what we can get."

I wipe tomato juice from my chin and say, "Is that where you were living before you came to Salinas?"

Valora's face darkens, so I glance at Mrs. Padilla. Her deep brown eyes glow golden-green.

My question has hurt them, and it makes me wonder. Who did they leave behind? Or are they running away from something? Someone?

"We can't talk about that," Valora says sternly. She's forgotten about the tortilla pinched between her fingers.

Mrs. Padilla presses a hand to her daughter's shoulder. "It's okay, m'ija. We can tell him."

"Mamá," Valora whispers, and switches to Spanish.

"It's okay." I wave a hand. "I don't need to know." I pop another chunk of tomato into my mouth. Backing away from a question is something I learned to do early on, especially with my older sister. Sometimes a man doesn't need to know the business of a woman. And many times he won't realize that until it's too late. I found this out the hard way when Vida aged into a woman. I'll just say this. Don't poke around the laundry basket of a girl who's become a woman. That's all I'm going to say.

I sense Valora's eyes on me. It's like she's noticing me for the first time, and the weight of her gaze ruffles my feathers. The heat from my chest moves to my cheeks.

Near the end of the meal, Abuelita says something in Spanish, but I can't catch the words. Not that it matters if I heard her clearly. Before I came today, I wrote out a list of words I remember from my Spanish language lessons. I counted out twelve.

"Abuelita wants to apologize for scaring you out there by the river," Valora translates between mouthfuls. Abuelita murmurs another sentence, and Valora adds. "She feels bad. She forgot that happens sometimes."

Valora blinks at her grandmother. She must be confused

like I am. Forgot *what* happens? That Abuelita's shapeshifting muddles the minds of anyone standing nearby? But Valora didn't seem to experience any effects from the green dust. Neither did Mrs. Padilla.

Valora tugs Abuelita's shawl and asks something in Spanish. I hope she's asking the same question burning up my thoughts. Why did Abuelita changing to human make me lose my mind?

Abuelita shakes her head and answers in Spanish.

Valora bobs her chin, musing over Abuelita's words. "Huh, is that true, Mamá?"

Mrs. Padilla shakes her head. "I don't know. That's new information to me."

I've lost track of this conversation, and it must be showing on my face because Valora tilts her head sideways and smirks. "Ay, Elbert." She laughs. "Look at his face, Mamá. He's so confused."

"M'ija," Mrs. Padilla gives a curt warning. "He's our guest."

Valora's back stiffens, and she droops her head to the side. Abuelita, sensing her granddaughter's chafed feelings, slips her an extra tortilla.

Mrs. Padilla smiles. "Abuelita says that when we change shape, a cloud of magical green dust poofs around us and protects us. The dust allows us to escape hunters and avoid watchful eyes while we change shape."

"That makes sense," I say, remembering the time the stag disappeared.

Mrs. Padilla rubs her chin like there's more. "She says some people react more strongly than others to the dust. She thinks it's because..."

"It's okay," I say. "I know I'm different."

Valora's gaze pokes me again.

Mrs. Padilla tilts her head. "She says the average person

gets a headache. They might temporarily go blind, get confused, but for us—our family—it's different. She thinks it's because we share the same type of magic." She touches Valora's and Abuelita's shoulders. "It comes from the earth, so the dust of Abuelita doesn't bother us. But your magic is fire." Mrs. Padilla shrugs. "I don't know. It's just not the same."

That's true. Our curses aren't the same. Their magic works with the plants and the earth. And I control fire. At least, that's what I should be doing. Most of the time, I'm just trying to avoid water.

My mind snags on that last thought. Water is my weakness. Maybe that means—

"Valora, can I see your burns?" I walk to her and kneel by her outstretched arms. Already, the burn marks have doubled in size, and black spots have formed over the wound.

"Ay, m'ija! Why didn't you say anything?" Mrs. Padilla joins my examination of Valora's arms.

"I didn't want to interrupt the conversation." She winces as Abuelita traces a finger lightly over the wound.

"I've never seen anything like this." Mrs. Padilla furrows her brow. "M'ija! Say something next time."

Valora pouts her lip and huffs. "Okay, okay."

Abuelita heads for the hut, most likely to grab bandages and ointments for Valora.

A thought crosses my mind. I wonder if Abuelita's dust is like when animals in nature use self-defense to ward off predators. Like skunks that spray foxes, or porcupines shooting quills.

Mrs. Padilla dismisses this thought with a wave of a hand. "No, no, Elbert. You are not a predator to us. You're our friend." She responds to something Abuelita says, then strokes Valora's hair, murmuring in Spanish.

Valora nudges her hand away and scowls. "Ay, Mamá. Don't fuss."

We wait in silence for Abuelita to prepare a healing salve, and Valora soon tires of our concern, so she tilts her head my way and says, "Did you finish?"

I blink. "Finish what?"

She swats at her mother, who has begun picking at the knots in her hair.

"Did you finish what you were saying before? About Abuelita's dust?"

"It's about our magic and how it works," I say. "Water is my weakness, but maybe you have a weakness too." I point my gaze at her blistered arms.

"Fire?" Valora murmurs, examining the red blotches on her skin. "But I haven't sparked yet."

Mrs. Padilla nods and rubs her chin, lost in thought. "But it will happen very soon, m'ija. Maybe Elbert is right. Maybe your body is preparing to spark."

Valora shakes her head. "Fire is dangerous to everyone. This is normal."

Then, as if to disagree, her body lurches forward and lands in my arms. She starts writhing like an earthworm caught in the sun. I sit in the dirt, holding Valora's convulsing body in my arms, not sure what to do. Abuelita dashes over and whispers something in Valora's ear. I hold on while Valora's body twists and shakes. Her fingers tug at my feathered skin.

"It's okay," I say, even as panic wells in my chest. I whisper as she twitches. "Breathe slowly. Breathe in. Breathe out. Try to stay calm."

Valora draws in a deep breath and exhales. I breathe with her.

Mrs. Padilla and Abuelita rush back to our side and kneel. Mrs. Padilla holds a wooden mixing bowl in her hands while Abuelita clutches an armful of torn cloths. They both start dabbing a dark paste onto Valora's raw skin. Valora flinches at first, but then her body relaxes. It takes a few minutes to apply the ointment. Then Abuelita wraps strips of cloth over Valora's arms.

Mrs. Padilla rises to her feet. "Think you can carry her inside, Elbert?"

Valora mumbles something in protest.

"M'ija!" Mrs. Padilla cringes. "Sorry, Elbert. Please ignore her."

Following her advice, I choose not to ask for a translation.

I tighten my grip around Valora and lift her off the ground. Her skin is warm and clammy, and her hair tickles my nose. I smell ginger and river water. She has slowed her breathing, and I hope she's not disgusted by my feathery arms and clumpy toes.

For a minute, I feel like I don't belong, like I don't deserve to hold her in my arms. I'm the reason she's injured, after all. Right then, Abuelita presses a hand against my back, easing me away from my self-loathing thoughts. I wonder if she knows how I'm feeling. Can she see it on my face?

I step inside their home, Valora still hanging off my neck.

"This way." Mrs. Padilla points to a pile of rumpled pillows and linens heaped in the corner. Abuelita smooths out the linens into a shape closer to that of a bed.

As I lower Valora onto the sheets, her dark, piercing eyes are wide, alert, and sour.

She'll be just fine.

I fumble for a blanket and brush my hand against a shirt.

Wait a minute. This is not a bed of linens, but a pile of worn-out clothes. And one of those shirts looks familiar.

"Is that...?" I catch myself before I finish the question. My old buttoned shirt, too tattered to hand down to Jorm, is tucked into the pile. Mrs. Padilla fidgets, clenching her jaw. She must know I recognize my shirt.

I glance away like I've stared at the sun for too long. This is wrong, peering into these women's lives. I haven't earned the right to meet this part of them.

A question gnaws at my mind: What are these women running from?

"I should go," I whisper and move to my feet.

Abuelita says something that sounds like protest, but Mrs. Padilla doesn't stop me. I cast one last glance.

Valora blinks at me from the bed. "What is it, Elbert?"

Abuelita inches toward me, reaching for my hand, but Mrs. Padilla's face sinks in shadows, her arms tightly crossed.

"Can I come back tomorrow?" I ask quietly.

Everyone waits for what Mrs. Padilla has to say.

She hesitates, and my chest tightens with every passing moment.

Finally, she sighs. "Of course, Elbert. Any time."

Chapter Eighteen

I pedal back home in the stillness of night. The swell of cricket chatter and dusty summer breezes comfort me as I ride without a thought. I should be anxious about how things ended with the Padillas, but I'm too tired to worry about that. Right now, the weeds crunching under my tires and the muddy scent of a slow-moving stream are the only things I dwell on. I keep pedaling, breathing in, breathing out, and listening to the dark. I ride this way for a while, easing my mind into nothing.

Until my tire hits a rock. My body launches into a scratchy pile of dead grass.

"Oompf!" says the rock.

Hmm. That's not a rock.

A soft sigh whispers from the lump shaped like a rock. I've heard this sigh many times. I'd die for that tubby little sigh.

I roll to my feet. "Finn?" I recognize his round cheeks in the starlight. His eyes are dull, like he's about to fall asleep.

Voices rise in the distance, calling out his name.

"What are you doing out here, buddy?"

He opens and closes his mouth like he's tasting the air.

"Finn," I say again, this time speaking from my gut. I grip him by the shoulders. "What are you doing?"

He flinches, and his eyes point to an empty space behind my shoulder. "She told me to come here."

I follow his gaze to dark stretches of grassy earth. Pinpricks of light bob in the distance, closer to the house. Pops must be sending out a search party.

"Is Juniper here?" Maybe I can convince Finn she wants to go home.

"She's always here," he says.

I reach for his hand. His skin is cold and damp. "What have you been doing? Did you go in the river?"

"This is a dream," Finn says as he shuffles through the weeds.

I slip my hands under his arms and twist. After I've rotated him toward home, I nudge him along. "Juni's this way." I wave in the direction of the glowing lights. "Hi, Juni! Oh, you want to go home? Sounds like a wonderful idea."

Finn groans, but he doesn't fight me. "That's not Juni. That's a bush."

For someone half-asleep, he's unusually aware of his surroundings.

We trudge through the brambles until a shadow swings a kerosene lamp in our faces. It's Jorm. He gasps, recognizing us both, then he does something I wasn't expecting. He grips his little brother by the arms and yells, "Finn!"

His frantic voice rattles me, and a sharp sting needles my chest as if the panic on Jorm's face has passed on to me.

"Easy, Jorm," I say, holding out a hand.

He ignores me, his eyes locked on Finn. "What are you doing? Stop coming out here!" Finn doesn't react, so Jorm jostles his shoulders and pats his cheek. "Are you still asleep? Wake up."

I touch Jorm's shoulder, but he jerks away. "No, Elbert,"

he seethes with wild eyes. He pinches Finn's cheeks. "You have to wake up!"

Mom abruptly appears, as if carried in with the breeze, and tugs Jorm away. Jorm kicks and spins free of Mom's grip, but he doesn't get far. Pops steps from the shadows, wraps an arm around him, and drags him through the dirt. Jorm writhes like a bag full of fire lizards.

"Wake him up, Pops. He has to wake up." Jorm's voice bends into a whine.

"He will, Son. He will," Pops says in his deep, sad voice.

These words seem to be what Jorm needs to hear because he stops his flailing and walks quietly, leaning on Pops.

As we near the house, Vida and Peto step out from the barn, sharing a lamp of their own. Trinna opens the door to the back porch, squints, and rubs her eyes. "Did Finn get out again?"

Mom snatches my arm as I walk by. "Elbert." Her voice is strained.

I didn't realize how upset she was. "Yes, Mom? Are you okay?"

"You can't be coming home this late." She clings to me as if a great wind is threatening to blow her away, and I'm the one keeping her feet on the ground.

Mom has never done this before, rely on me like this. I'm lost for words. I should reassure her that I will never come home this late, especially not with a little, half-sleeping brother exploring the dark. I should be quick to apologize and make promises, but instead, a prickling anger gathers in my chest. It grows stronger, deeper.

"Okay," I mutter.

Finn, still drowsy, is now closer to awake than asleep. He shuffles up the porch steps, and Jorm sniffles beside him, guiding Finn with his hand. Tears roll past his fog-stained glasses. "Wake up, Finn," he whispers.

"Why's Jorm crying? Why'd he tell Finn to wake up?" Trinna whispers next to Mom.

Wake up.

Jorm's words tug at the back of my mind where I keep my oldest memories. I've heard these words before. Back in a time I've nearly forgotten.

Trinna's probing questions and Mom's hushed voice only result in Jorm clenching his fists and sucking in breaths. I can see bitterness grow in his pinched eyes. I know this look because it reminds me of my own sour feelings. Every time I catch Finn sleepwalking in the dark, first comes panic—What if I don't catch him this time? What if he falls into the river? What if he gets attacked by a wild animal?

What if our family loses another one of us?

Just the idea stirs a sour feeling inside my gut, a bitter taste in my mouth. I lost my sister before I was old enough to protect her. I was too young to do anything. Too useless. Now, I'm old enough to protect Finn, but one day, I might not be there in time to catch him. That makes me scared.

I bet Jorm feels the same way.

"Peto," I say to my older brother as he passes.

"Yep?"

I'm not sure how to say this. Normally, I knock heads with Jorm because he's my annoying little brother, but tonight is different. Tonight, the kindness of siblings is necessary. And deep down, I know it's my turn to be kind. But if I ask Jorm to sit with me, he'll ignore me. Maybe, if Peto is with us...

Peto follows my gaze.

"Ah," he says, nodding slowly. "Jorm! Over here, buddy."

Jorm walks over and sniffles by the door. "What?"

Peto sits on the edge of the porch. "We just want to ask you something."

When he says "we," I join my older brother sitting on the porch and stare at the dark sky. I can sense Jorm standing there behind us, breathing and scratching his head. A fire lizard scuttles past my toes, and a bat whips behind the arching shadow of the oak tree. We sit with the night while Jorm fidgets behind us, no doubt questioning my presence.

Finally, the wooden porch shifts as my younger brother sits between us.

"You okay, Jorm?" I try to keep my tone short and unbothered. He wouldn't want me to care too much about the tears dripping off his face. To be extra careful, I avoid his eyes.

"What are you thinking about, buddy?" Peto's baritone voice rumbles.

Jorm sighs heavily, like an old man, and stays quiet.

Does he need us to repeat the question? I don't know. Peto doesn't seem worried. In fact, if I didn't know better, I'd say he's asleep.

Finally, Jorm speaks. "Juniper."

I keep my voice light. "You're thinking about her? Why's that?" I don't want to sound too gentle or concerned. He wouldn't want me to act like Mom.

Jorm rubs his cheek with his knuckle and chooses not to answer. I twiddle my thumbs while Peto exhales.

The waiting works, because after a few long, dragging moments of silence, Jorm speaks. "Sometimes, I don't know— I just don't understand. Why didn't she stay with us?"

That's a good question. Why *didn't* Juniper stay with us?

Peto replies first. "Well, it's hard to know these things. Especially when we're living this side of heaven."

"Do you remember her?" I ask Jorm. We were all pretty young when Juni was still with us. About five or six years ago now.

Jorm nods. "I remember."

We pull out the memory of our sister like an old bedtime

story. As we're sharing, the tightness in my chest slowly loosens. And when my breathing comes easily again, I remember.

Chapter Nineteen

I remember how it felt to have Juniper as part of the family. "Our little blessing." That's what Mom called her growing belly. That was before we knew she was growing twins: Finn and Juniper. Finn came to us the night of June twelfth, then Juniper joined a few minutes later into the dawn of June thirteenth.

I was just a boy, about Jorm's age now. At this point, I've forgotten some things, but there are spots of memories that still burn in my mind. One of these memories is the first few weeks after Juniper and Finn entered the world. Strangers came to the house every day with gifts of food—minced pies, roasted potatoes and beans, a dish of spiced apples and ham, and trinkets for the "little big ones"—Trinna, Jorm, and me. I remember one family dropping off a fully plucked chicken ready for scalding.

Pops was a mess. He fumbled in the kitchen until Vida took it upon herself to learn how to cook. A few days after that, the stench of unwashed clothes, most of them soiled infant diapers, could not be ignored. That's when I was assigned my first "big boy" chore: laundry.

Mom spent all of her time with Finn and Juniper, appeasing them, feeding, changing, bathing, and all sorts of other things. By the time moonlight climbed through the window, her face would pucker with exhaustion, but she had a glow in her eyes.

"This is good work, Elbert," she'd reassure me whenever I complained about how tired she was. Then she'd pile two wailing babies on me. Often, something warm pooled on the tops of my legs. Time for more laundry.

Life demanded a lot from us in those days. It was exhausting, but our guts were filled with laughter, and each night we slept like bears in the winter. Mornings were like spring. We'd rise with aching limbs from our slumber. And we'd be hungry.

Just over two years. That's how long we had Juniper. And in one night, we lost her.

I don't know how the fire started. If anyone knows, no one has told me. It could have been a spark that popped from the hearth. It could have been a candle dribbling off balance until it rolled sideways. It could have been the spit of a fire lizard, spooked by a shadow.

I don't know. I just remember Peto wrenching me awake. An orange glimmer warmed his face, and the bite of smoke was already scratching my lungs. He didn't say anything. He just tugged a shirt over my arms and handed me a pair of pants —his pants.

He helped Jorm dress, too, and then he said, "This way."

By the time we ran barefoot on the lawn, boots in our arms, Vida and Trinna were already outside, shivering against the Arkansas breeze. Peto moved to fill a pail with water, but Mom stopped him. It was too late for that.

This next part I'd forgotten until now. Maybe because I didn't understand it at the time. I must have told myself it was just a trick of the eyes, an illusion. But now I know better. Now I know who Pops really is.

First off, Pops was still inside. The house glowed orange like a wood stove. How could he still be in there? And Juniper and Finn—where were they?

Pops burst through the burning door carrying Finn and Juniper in the folds of his arms. A blanket of flames burned his back and shoulders. But wait... That's not how it was. Those flames weren't burning the clothes on his back. They were enveloping him. They were coming *from* him. Wings of fire spilling from his shoulders. This must be magic. Pops must be an angel.

Mom appeared beside us. The weight of her arms trembled against my shoulder as she tugged Trinna, Jorm, and me into a circle. We were so young back then, too small to do anything. I remember feeling so useless. There was nothing I could do but watch, and Mom wouldn't even let me do that.

We pressed our foreheads together, and I closed my eyes. Even as Mom held us firmly in place, I felt my world slipping —*changing*. And I wished against the fire.

Don't take my home away. Just leave us alone.

It was a useless wish. I wasn't going to save anything—or anyone—that day.

Finally, I looked over at our house, now black and broken. The fire was gone, so was Juniper, and there was nothing I could do about it.

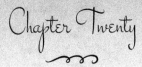

Chapter Twenty

I've been rising before dawn to plow through my early morning chores so I can leave the farm earlier and return before dusk. Mornings have been lonely. Finn and Trinna don't follow me around like they used to. Maybe they're getting too old for that. Since our conversation on the porch, Jorm has acknowledged me in passing, usually with a curt nod. The hard glint in his eye has softened.

Today, I finish my midday meal and snag a bike. Finn stares as I wheel past. He clutches one of the chicks to his chest and sighs. I know I should wave to him as I ride toward the river. I should reassure him. I will come back. But something holds my tongue and turns my arms to stone. As I choose silence over kindness, a sourness lingers in my mouth.

I just hope that when I've climbed past this part of my life, his tubby face will forgive me.

I pedal alongside the dwindling river, clutching a bag full of glass jars filled with water. Only a couple of weeks have passed since I first saw Valora floating on the river with Abuelita in crocodile form. Back then, the waters had spread wide, but shallow. Now, the stream has been reduced to a rocky layer of mud. A trickle marches north, weaving its way through the stones and dead branches.

According to my earth science lessons, the river never leaves us, it just sinks underground. When I mentioned this to Mrs. Padilla and Abuelita, they used magic to carve a muddy hole in the riverbed, but the water was too stagnant for drinking, which is why I'm lugging this bagful of jars filled with fresh water.

When I arrive at the Padilla women's home, I notice their hut has doubled in size since I first saw it. They've attached new pieces of scavenged lumber, stones, and their own signature twisting vines.

I catch sight of Valora's dark hair. She's bending over a clump of vegetables in the garden. I *do* find it suspicious how their garden shares the same sort of fruits and vegetables as ours—carrots, squash, tomatoes, peach and lemon saplings, and most recently, strawberries.

Yes. Very suspicious. If Valora is just now planting strawberries, maybe she was telling the truth. She wasn't the one who planted them in our garden. None of us have touched the berries, even as they mature and plump. I can't speak for the others, but for me, seeing the fruit makes me think of Juni, and I don't want them to disappear.

Mrs. Padilla sticks her head out of the hut's opening and grins. "Elbert! Good to see you again."

I wave back awkwardly until Abuelita comes up and pinches my arm. "Hola, m'ijo," she says with a scowl, then smiles warmly.

Valora walks over and cups a hand to her forehead, shading her eyes from the sun. "What are you doing here?" She stares like I owe her money. I wince, glimpsing the scars wrapping her wrists. Evidence of the night I burned her.

Mrs. Padilla walks up to me and squeezes my shoulder. "Let's go to the hills today," she says and runs behind the hut to shift into a wolf. I wait for the wind to sweep away the glittering green cloud while Valora climbs the wolf's shaggy flank and clings to the back of her neck.

Then we run.

They're much faster than me, but I'm not too far behind. I've learned a lot since my first day with the Padillas. I've learned to focus on the fire burning in my chest. I coax it from its hiding place and use it to light my shoulders and arms. This adds to my strength as I force my way through windswept hilltops. But I have to restrain myself so that fire doesn't trail down my legs. That would be dangerous, especially with how dry the hills have become these past couple of months.

We gallop over inclines and slide down slopes for close to half an hour. Then we pause on a golden summit where the wind ruffles my feathers. The Spreckels sugar beet factory is northeast of us, bustling with field workers and horse-drawn plows combing acres of soil. The vibrant farmland carves a green path through the yellowing valley, stopping shy of the river.

"Okay, back up now, Elbert," Valora says.

I scramble to a safe distance and wait for Mrs. Padilla to open her massive jaws and spill a burst of green light. The wind pushes the cloud of dust aside while I stay safe out of nose's reach. When the dust clears, Mrs. Padilla is walking toward Valora in human form, golden weeds tangled in her hair.

"Now, that's the goal, Elbert," she calls while I climb back up the hill. "Transform yourself into the nature of your magic —and then back to your human nature."

When Valora suggested the idea early on, it felt so true. "If we can change from human to animal and back again, maybe Elbert can change, too."

And back again. If I could finish shifting into the phoenix, then maybe I could shift back.

121

I considered talking to Pops about this curse, but I still remember the night he said he didn't understand what was happening to me, and I believe him. The most he has changed was the night he pulled Finn and Juniper from the fire. The flaming wings arching over him were impressive, but I don't remember any feathers. Or bird-like toes.

Mrs. Padilla points to my taloned feet and downy arms. "Stop focusing on your body like it's a mistake."

But it *is* a mistake. A huge one. Of course, I don't say this out loud.

Mrs. Padilla goes on to describe the process of transforming. Again.

"Focus on your inner breathing." She closes her eyes. "Imagine drawing breath from your gut. Imagine the fire in your chest passing through the veins in your arms to the points of your fingers until your hands glow."

I've followed her steps, the breathing, eyes closed, the mental focus. I must have tried for hours before I harnessed a spark into a flame with confidence and control. Then it was a few days more before I could take that flame and contain it to just my arms and upper back. After that, I practiced pulling patches of fire from burning brush and grinding them into the dirt.

But I still can't change into a firebird. Not that I want to. As far as I know, I will have to if I want to get rid of these feathers.

I breathe deeply and lie to myself. I'm not a mistake. As I go through the steps, I imagine embracing the phoenix side of me, this firebird that has ruined my life.

No. This is my life now. I am not just part firebird. I am *full* firebird. To change back to human, I must first finish changing into the phoenix. I must finish this half-finished spell.

"Mamá." Valora's whisper breaks my concentration. "I see him."

I follow her gaze to the base of the hill and spot a beast I thought I'd never see again.

"Do you know him?" The back of my neck prickles. The beast looks exactly like Mr. Deer, the stag that saved Finn from a pile of fire lizards. A beast much larger than the average size of its species, with intelligent eyes that reach for your soul. Eyes like a human.

"No," Valora says quickly. A tear glistens on her cheek. "That's just a beast in a field." More tears slip from her eyes as she stares at Mr. Deer fidgeting near a withered bush.

I join Mrs. Padilla as she crouches to the ground and observes the stag saunter past the brambles. His coat is the color of rust and dead grass, and his antlers sweep the dirt as he picks at the worn-out weeds, searching for something green.

"We've been watching him," Mrs. Padilla says. "These past couple months, he's been lingering in the hills mostly, staying out of people's way. We give him food if we can. We grow grasses." She opens the drawstring of a pouch hanging at her hip, digs out a handful of seeds, and drops them on a dusty patch of earth. She then presses her palms on the seeds. A green glow spills out between her fingers, and when she lifts her hand, a bed of grass slowly peaks through the dust. "But we have to keep coming back and growing more patches of grass. We don't want him migrating toward the mountains. We're keeping him here until we..." Mrs. Padilla's voice fades on the last word.

"Until we figure out how to change him back," Valora finishes for her. "He's been lost to his wild form, and we're not sure how to bring him back to human."

"What's his name?" I hope I'm not asking too much. I know they've avoided telling me this.

Mrs. Padilla rubs her chin and opens her mouth. Just a squeak comes out.

"I'll say it," Valora slips a hand under her mother's arm, and her eyes lock onto mine. "His name is Andrés. He is my brother."

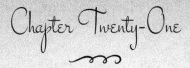

Chapter Twenty-One

Andrés the stag twitches his head upright as if responding to his name. He lopes across the golden grasses until he weaves into a glen, fringed with evergreens.

I have so many questions weighing down my tongue, but I only allow myself to ask one. "How did this happen?"

Valora flexes her jaw and shakes her head. "That's a big question," she says.

"M'ijo, there's so much—most of it, I shouldn't say," Mrs. Padilla says. She rubs both eyes with one hand. "We're here because we followed him. We're protecting him."

So, the women aren't running from someone as I'd thought. But if they're protecting him, maybe that means—

"Is Andrés running from someone?" I say cautiously.

Valora's body stiffens.

Mrs. Padilla closes her eyes before answering. "We haven't been followed here. Not yet."

Not the most confident of answers. I knew this conversation was painful for them, but I have to ask. "Is he running from a photographer from San Francisco? Mr. Halifax?"

Valora mulls over this question, then gasps suddenly. "Ah! Mamá, he's talking about Gordo."

They both laugh. Then Mrs. Padilla clears her throat, suppressing another chuckle. "We probably shouldn't call him that. We know his name. We knew it already."

A smug expression tugs at Valora's lips. "He introduced himself to us, yes. Tried to chat, but we refused, of course."

I swallow. Not sure what to say next, but I have to let them know. "Okay, I have two things I need to tell you right now."

Both women snap their eyes at me. "What is it?" Mrs. Padilla's voice sharpens.

I smile nervously. "Mr. Halifax has been collecting news clippings of you. And... researching you. I found a book. Something about shapeshifting?"

Mrs. Padilla rubs her forehead and hisses like a snake. "M'ijo, I wish you'd said something sooner."

My head droops down. "Yeah, I'm sorry."

I'm an idiot. Of course, I should have told them right away. Mr. Halifax was *researching* them.

Mrs. Padilla squeezes my shoulder. "Don't worry. We'll forgive you."

"Maybe not today," Valora adds.

"Yes, probably not today." Mrs. Padilla grins. "Soon. Before your next birthday, I promise."

I squinch my face and wheeze a laugh.

Valora grips my arm. The simple gesture makes my skin prickle. "Don't ever forget to tell us something like that again." Her words are like frigid water sliding down my neck.

I nod. Then I remember something else, and I clear my throat. "So... I have one more thing to tell you."

Mrs. Padilla's eyes burn like embers.

"What is it, Pollo?" Valora says.

The way she says Pollo. She sounds annoyed.

"I saw your brother a couple months ago. In June," I say.

"I'm pretty sure he transformed into a human. Right after Mr. Halifax took a photo."

"He took a photo?" Valora's face pales. "No!"

"But that means Andrés shifted to human in June." Mrs. Padilla speaks over Valora's cry. "He hasn't been a stag as long as we thought." Hope sparks in her eyes, but then her face tightens. "That also means Mr. Halifax has evidence of us shifting."

Valora grunts. "Are we going to knock him senseless and send him on the next train to México?"

"M'ija! Why'd you say something like that?" Mrs. Padilla's eyes widen at me, like she's worried this dark side of her daughter wasn't already obvious.

She did whack me with a shovel once. Her words do not surprise me.

"He's a terrible man, yes," Mrs. Padilla admits. "But not like..." She whispers the last part in Spanish.

"Can Elbert do it, then?" Valora points an eyebrow at me.

"Do what, my darling?" Mrs. Padilla sneaks me a tired smile.

Valora inhales and presses her lips together. We all know what she's about to say.

"No, I'm not going to kidnap a man," I answer before she can ask.

Valora pouts at this news. Then her eyebrows sag. "We're going to leave again, aren't we?"

Mrs. Padilla ignores the question, or maybe she's not sure what the answer should be. "I wish you'd said this sooner."

My stomach churns. Is this what it's like to fail someone? Mrs. Padilla's anger reminds me of *my* anger with Pops when I found out the secrets he'd been hiding.

"Please don't go," I whisper. "I'm so sorry. I should have told you about this sooner. Please, stay."

Valora bites her lower lip while Mrs. Padilla's eyes dart

back and forth, no doubt gathering a plan. She rests a hand lightly on my arm. "If we stay, we need you to tell us if anyone comes to town. Any outsider acting suspicious, you tell us immediately. No matter what you're doing. They could be a trapper."

"Of course," I promise. I wait for their faces to relax before asking my next question. "What's a trapper?"

Mrs. Padilla doesn't answer my question right away. Instead, she leads us back to the hut. Abuelita is waiting for us with freshly peeled hard-boiled eggs and a pot of beans seasoned with cilantro and chili. We munch on our food outside by the garden, and when our bellies are full, I venture back to our conversation from earlier.

"So, when you say 'trapper,' do you mean a fur trapper?" My great uncle was a fur trapper in his youth, but I don't know about anyone doing it as a business, not recently.

"No, not at all. Trappers are hired to hunt down and trap a specific beast, usually a rare one," Mrs. Padilla says, while scooping a bite of egg into her mouth.

"Who hired these trappers?" I try to keep my voice casual. This is the secret these women cling to. Normally, I'd let them keep their secrets, but there's a problem. If they're running from someone, chances are, *I* should run, too.

All three women respond with silence, so I switch to a different question, hoping to dig out *some* answers. "How many shapeshifters are there? How many trappers? I didn't realize this was so—widespread. I thought you were the only family who had this ability."

Mrs. Padilla shakes her head. "We're definitely not the only shapeshifters—as you know."

Ah, that's right. *I'm* a shapeshifter. It's just hard to believe when I've never successfully shifted.

"But there aren't many of us left—not many that use earth magic, anyway. I don't know about fire magic people. People like you. But some earth magic people live in México, on the outskirts of villages. We hide our abilities from the village folk. As for the trappers, it's hard to say how many. Abuelita?"

Mrs. Padilla speaks Spanish to the older woman, and Abuelita gives a short answer.

"Es verdad?" Mrs. Padilla says.

Valora folds her arms and shivers. "I didn't know *that*," she says.

"What is it?" I say, shifting my gaze between all three women.

Valora flexes her jaw before she answers. "Abuelita says trappers are like shapeshifters. They pass down their abilities and secrets to their children."

My breath catches in my throat as two words ring loudly in my ears: Abilities. *Secrets.*

What?

"Does that mean they also use magic?" My voice sounds weak to my ears.

Abuelita speaks again, her eyes locking onto mine. I fight the urge to interrupt and ask for a translation.

"They don't use magic," Valora speaks for her grandmother. "Trappers hunt us down, but they do this with special weapons, secret ones..." She pauses for Abuelita to say more. "... always made of metal, powered by steam—and electricity."

"And you've been hiding from these trappers all this time?" Other questions pop into my mind. Questions like, why have they been in Salinas for this long when they probably should have left weeks ago?

"We haven't been hiding. Not exactly," Mrs. Padilla says firmly, as if closing a door on this part of the conversation.

I choose to nudge her forward, for my own sake. For theirs. "I know there's something you don't want to tell me, but please remember who I am. If these trappers are coming for you, they'll come for me, too."

Mrs. Padilla shakes her head. "They have a strict code. Trappers only target those with a mark on them."

Valora throws up her hands. "Ay, Mamá! Let's just tell him all of it."

"No, m'ija." Mrs. Padilla shoots her daughter a glare and speaks a few choice words in Spanish.

"Elberto," Abuelita says, motioning me close. She whispers in my ear, "Is... Andrés. Andrés," she gestures her hands like she's conjuring words, "tiene un... mark."

My scalp quivers as I piece together Abuelita's words. There's a mark on *Andrés*.

"Did Andrés do something? Why does he have a mark?" My question halts the chattering between Mrs. Padilla and her daughter. They throw fiery glares at Abuelita.

"He did nothing." Valora's voice cracks with anger. "He's the sweetest boy. Wouldn't hurt a gnat."

Mrs. Padilla sighs. "We don't know for sure if he's been marked. Back home, Andrés shifted to a stag and wandered onto an estate in the middle of the day—in plain sight." Her words are heavy, like she's forcing them out of her mouth. "But this estate belonged to a very powerful landlord. He chased Andrés outside of town with a gun and a team of marksmen, but Andrés never stopped running, even after they lost his trail. We followed him north, all the way up here, and then Andrés just stopped. It's like he decided Salinas is his home."

"Maybe the man just wanted Andrés out of town," I say.

Mrs. Padilla does not look convinced. "Maybe, Elbert. You could be right. But we didn't stay long enough to find out."

Valora clasps her mother's hand. "It's okay, Mamá. We *had* to run."

Mrs. Padilla's eyebrows pinch together. "I should have stayed. I could have convinced them Andrés was just a trick of the eye, just an oversized grizzly wandering between trees."

"It usually works." Valora glances over. "People have a hard time believing in magic."

I think of Leo and nod. It's true.

So, this is who they've been running from all this time? The *possibility* of a trapper hired by a stranger tracking them across the country?

How long will they run from a ghost?

Even with all this new information, something still does not make sense. "Why would Andrés go near a man like that?"

Mrs. Padilla grimaces and nods. "In some ways, Andrés is unique. We can't just tell him *not* to do things, even dangerous things like shifting in public. He won't listen."

"Andrés does what he wants," Valora adds. "But it's not like he's being rebellious. It's more like he doesn't understand why he shouldn't do certain things. He's always been this way."

"We worry because he's still so new to shifting," Mrs. Padilla says. "The longer he stays in animal form, the more likely he'll lose his mind, turn wild, and forget he was ever human. But you say he shifted back in June. I hope that means he's still holding on to his human side."

A heavy silence settles over us.

I wait for a bit, and then I ask, "If a trapper could be any stranger coming through town, how will I know which one is him?"

Mrs. Padilla tugs my hand into hers. Her eyes glow like emerald fire. "How does the rabbit know the coyote is following her?" She taps my chest. "You'll sense it here, Elbert. That's how you'll know."

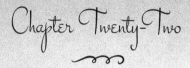

Chapter Twenty-Two

Trappers could show up any day now, and if anyone knows anything about strangers creeping through town, it will be Leo. On my next trip to town, I mosey around Leo's shop, hoping he'll spill some gossip.

I don't want to gossip with other ears nearby, so I linger next to Leo's family portrait. I wait for a batch of red-headed folks—a man, woman, and girl my age—to finish shopping. They gawk at my feathered face, especially the young girl— most likely the man and woman's daughter. She stares at me, unblinking as they approach Leo for their purchase. I lean forward and scowl until she returns to her parents.

Leo tries selling them his latest inventions—binoculars for "spying giant beasts" and an iron whistle to "lure the beasts out of hiding." He waves to me as the family brushes past, and an uneasy chill squeezes my stomach, reminding me of my mission: root out the strangers in town.

"How's everyone doing?" Leo says while tugging out the pipe behind his ear. "And your livestock? They okay?"

"Alive and well-taken care of," I say as I drop a tuft of fire onto the tobacco for him. "Are there more rabies cases?"

Leo sighs. "Yes, unfortunately. The Campbells had to put down their dog last week. And some of the cattle at Spreckels have shown signs of the disease. Some people think it's those giant beasts."

I don't want to linger on the suspicions surrounding the Padilla family, so I say, "Any new gossip?"

He cracks a grin and speaks freely, like a barrel of wine with its stopper removed. He starts with his list of budding romances.

"Vida and Daichi. Beautiful couple, but the town doesn't like a white woman talking to a Japanese man." Leo shakes his head. "Two races and two religions don't mix—that's what the religious folk say."

This news surprises and stings me. I'd always imagined Daichi and Vida starting a life together.

"What religion is Daichi?"

"Well, he's a man, not a religion," Leo chuckles at his own joke. "But as for Japanese religions, I've heard people say words like 'Shinto' and 'Buddhist,' I think. But I don't know what they mean."

"Hmm, me neither."

He goes on about the most recent obituaries and the latest pregnancy announcements. But when it comes to strangers, he scratches his forehead. "Oh, well there's always the next load of seasonal hires at Spreckels. But you know how that goes."

I do know how it goes. A rush of new faces, usually lone travelers like Daichi, or the occasional family, sweep into town and fill up the local hotels or pitch tents outside the fields. I forgot about this. It would be easy for trappers to blend in with the Spreckels crowd.

"Oh, but there's one more thing," he adds. "Harold's looking for his cow again."

🔥

I report my findings to Valora later that same day.

"New hires?" She wrinkles her nose. "I'll tell Mamá."

I'm afraid to ask, but I say it anyway. "Does that mean you have to leave?"

"I don't know. Maybe. If we can convince Andrés to come with us," she says.

We're lying flat on our bellies on the crest of a shaggy hill, keeping an eye on the stag. At a short distance, he stoops low, gnawing on a crop of magically grown clovers sprinkled over a patch of grass—Mrs. Padilla's home-grown meal for him. The stalks of grass are thick as ribbons and greener than rain-soaked moss. The sight of it almost makes *me* hungry.

Valora touches my forearm lightly. "Thank you for your help."

"You're welcome." I hold her gaze and grin.

Red splotches pool on her cheeks, and she twists away.

"Has he been staying out of trouble?" I point a thumb at Andrés.

She sighs. "He's been staying clear of town during the day. Except for the occasional hunting trap, no one has bothered him."

"Someone's been setting traps?"

"Yes," she says. "But they're too small to damage him. His hooves crush them whenever he steps on one."

"Wow! That's very dangerous to everyone else. Are they by the river?"

"Ah, let's see." She ticks off fingers. "Two in the hills, three by the river."

"That's awful. Maybe I can ask around town and find out who's setting those traps."

She shrugs. "It's not that bad. We steal the catches sometimes. Lately, rabbits and squirrels."

That's one way to make the best of a situation.

"What about your mom? Has she been more careful lately

when she shifts to the wolf?" I laugh, remembering the time I caught them in the garden, but Valora is quiet. I rub my temples, hoping my last statement hasn't offended her.

"It was really hard when we first got here," she says. "We had nothing. No food, no money—nothing. And women traveling alone, *Mexicana* women, that can be dangerous. So, Mamá shifted into the wolf sometimes to search for food because it felt safer. This is how we survive."

I never thought about this before—the dangers of women traveling alone.

Her piercing eyes wander back to mine. "What are you thinking about?"

I scratch the feathers on the back of my neck. "Um, I was just thinking about how I wish..." My cheeks burst into flames —at least, this is how it feels.

She grins like she's uncovered one of my secrets. "Your eyes are glowing orange. What are you *thinking*, Pollo?"

That pink color is back in her cheeks.

I smile as heat radiates from my face. "I'm thinking I need to protect you."

It's funny because it isn't true. She's got a wolf and an alligator at her fingertips. Plus, she's days away from shifting into her own fearsome beast.

She cocks her head sideways. "Maybe one day, Pollo, I will let you do that."

"I'm counting on it," I say and lean toward her.

"Ay, Elbert. Too close." She pushes my shoulder, but not that hard. She turns away, clearly flustered.

I like the way she grins at me, as if I'm not really too close. But I shrug and give her some space.

"Which animal do you want to be?" I say.

She purses her lips, her eyes lost in thought. "I don't know yet. I don't have to decide right away. It takes time for my body to decide."

What an interesting thought. To choose what you turn into. That is one big difference between the Padilla family and myself.

She exhales, probably still pondering my question, and whispers something so quietly, I'm not sure if I'm supposed to hear it. "If I could choose, I'd be a jaguar."

I glance back at Andrés. He's rifling through the rest of his meal, then his ear twitches to the left. He swings his neck upright. I sit up, too, and scan the hills. Has he noticed something? Thoughts of trappers slink into my mind.

I grab Valora's hand. "I hear something." I listen harder. Sounds like an animal braying—and a soft clinking sound.

Valora leaps to her feet. "Where?"

I hold my breath, waiting for more sounds to reach my ears. Andrés bolts forward, clearly just as curious as we are, but he's heading toward town. toward the highway.

"Andrés!" Valora shrieks.

We skid down a slope and race toward the source of the bellowing. The creature sounds like it's in pain, whatever it is.

I pray silently as I run. Please, don't let Andrés run into the highway.

I lose sight of Andrés as we round a hedge of cypress trees. He must have darted into a clump of trees. Hopefully, he'll stay put.

Valora and I keep walking until we find a creature panting and bellowing on the ground. Slumped over the creature is Harold.

"Chewbie!" I shriek and skid to her side.

Harold jumps back. "What are you doing here?"

I ignore him and lean over my trusty friend. She lifts her head and stares at me with dark, liquid eyes, then she sags back to the ground.

"She's sick," Harold says. "Rabies, probably."

My heart hammers in my ears. Not Chewbie.

"She'll be okay, won't she?" My throat tightens because I know better. She won't be okay. No animal or human is ever okay after this type of disease attacks their bodies.

Harold scoffs. "I can't believe you would ask that." He shakes his head. "Especially when it's creatures like *you* who made her sick."

He must be joking. Why would I ever make Chewbie sick? How could I?

"Who told you that?" I say.

His eyes flash, and he glances to the side. "Everyone says it."

"You know that's not true," I say.

"Chewbie wasn't the first animal to get sick, but everyone agrees the sickness didn't spread until after those giant beasts arrived—and after you changed into *this.*"

Chewbie moans, pulling us back to her. A stream of drool dribbles down her bottom lip.

"Come on, Chewbie," I say, fighting back the force of emotions swirling through me. I could never do this to her.

Or could I?

I don't fully understand my powers, and we haven't been watching Andrés that carefully. He could have been spreading this disease to other creatures when he's roaming alone.

Could this be my fault?

Sadness and anger grip me by the throat. When I speak, my voice comes out as a gasp. "Chewbie, hang on. I'll find a cure."

"There is no cure," Harold shouts, inches from my face.

No cure. The words crack against my chest. My worst fear. Is this true? Is there no cure for Chewbie?

A deep ache stirs in my gut, reminding me that there's also no cure for my curse. Curse or no curse. I just wish this sadness would untangle from my chest. Is there really no cure?

"Aggh!" Harold shrieks and leaps to his feet. He holds up

trembling hands and backs away from Chewbie, his eyes caught on something behind me.

I swivel back and catch Andrés crunching through the weeds. His golden-green eyes flicker. So much for staying out of sight. That's when I realize I've lost sight of Valora. This is good. She should be hidden away. She doesn't need Harold asking questions.

"No, Andrés!" she screams, announcing her presence to Harold. I should have known she'd come out of hiding to stop her stubborn stag-of-a-brother.

He sweeps his antlers at his sister, lifts her into the air, and flings her into the arms of a tree.

"Andrés!" she sputters, scrambling her way back to the ground.

Harold watches all of this, speechless.

The stag bends down and inspects Chewbie's panting body. Valora claws her way back to the ground and springs toward the stag. I hook an arm around her waist and drag her behind a bush. She scratches at me, but I hold onto her shoulders. "What are you doing?" I say. "He'll see you!"

"Go away." Harold's voice cuts in. He's pushing Andrés's side. The stag doesn't move, but resumes sniffing Chewbie's face.

"You go," I plead, gripping her hands in mine. "Tell your mom what's happening. I'll get Andrés out of here."

"No! It's too late. Flaco already saw me." She narrows her eyes. "Today is not the day I let you protect me, Pollo."

Flaco. Is this a nickname for Harold? A twinge of jealousy works its way to my chest. I hope "flaco" doesn't mean "handsome."

She breaks from my grip just before a green pile of smoke spills over our heads. I dart backward until I'm safely out of reach.

Did Andrés just shift to a human?

I gulp in fresh air, pinch my nose, and step into the haze.

All I see are shadows at first, then as I step closer, I spot Valora standing near Harold. Chewbie is lying flat on the ground, and next to her is Andrés. He's not a hulking stag anymore, but a boy with scraggly hair and scrappy pants. He hovers a hand over the cow's head and waits. A soft, green glow collects underneath his palm, then he presses his hand against Chewbie's forehead. She twitches and bellows softly. Then she relaxes.

"Chewbie!" Harold cries.

My eyes sting, and pressure builds in the back of my throat.

I need to breathe. How long has it been? Two minutes? I dash to a safe distance and drink in the fresh air. As I wait for the winds to brush away the haze, Andrés, back to stag form, breaks through the line of trees and gallops toward the hills. Valora screams after him, shaking her fist in the air. She keeps running even after he bounds over the rise and out of sight.

I walk over to Harold, stepping lightly. He's hunched over Chewbie with tears smearing the dirt on his cheeks.

I gulp in a breath and whisper, "Is she okay?"

He grimaces and nods. "She'll be okay."

A heavy weight slides off my chest, and a fresh batch of tears blur my vision. Andrés *cured* Chewbie. I didn't know he could do that. Did any of the Padilla women know?

"Who was that girl?" Harold says.

That's right. Harold saw Valora. He saw Andrés change into a human and back to a stag. I have to be careful with what I say next. Maybe I should threaten him to keep silent.

"No one," I say.

"Well," Harold digs a toe in the dirt. He catches my gaze with his watery eyes. "If you see her or that boy again, please thank them for me."

Chapter Twenty-Three

People are talking about Andrés. Not exactly *bad* things. He's been roaming closer to the farms, usually early in the morning. One of the Cooper sons glimpsed giant antlers bounding in the morning gloom. A trail of large hoof prints cut straight from the stables and headed east. The oldest Cooper boy ran to check on his horses, fearing the worst. He found a surprise instead.

One of the horses in the stable, a mare showing early signs of rabies, sprang to her feet and headed to the water trough, unbothered. Cured. Then someone else caught sight of Andrés dashing into the fields at dusk. He left behind one of the neighborhood mutts—Spike. He'd been frothing at the mouth and snarling for days. According to Leo, he's as good as new. Completely cured of the disease.

There's another story circling, too, about a "magnificent beast" scooping a barnyard kitten from a lofty branch and lowering it to safety. I think the kitten was ordinary, though. Not diseased. So, Andrés was just doing a good deed there.

There hasn't been a rabies outbreak for days now, and people have been talking. Maybe the giant stag has got something to do with it. No one will say how he cures these animals —with magic. I don't blame them. As far as my town is concerned, magic doesn't exist.

I've been thinking about Andrés and all his good deeds. I remember the time he scraped those fire lizards off Finn's belly. I think Andrés was helping Finn on purpose. And he did help him. He saved Finn's life.

I've decided I'll do anything to stop these trappers from catching Andrés. He saved one of mine. Now, I'll return the favor. But there's a problem. I need to know more about these trappers, and the only person who's met one is Abuelita, who doesn't like talking about them—in English or Spanish.

Valora already told me everything she knows. She said that a few generations ago, back when trappers had more shapeshifters to hunt, trappers were common in the southern part of California, especially inside the border of Mexico. A lone trapper, a man of Spanish descent, chased Abuelita from her Mexican village across the border to California. When I asked what happened to the trapper, I learned Abuelita turned to alligator form and slashed the man's steam-powered weapon from his hands. Killed him with one chomp. That's how Valora tells it, anyway.

I want to know more about the trapper weapons, but Valora doesn't know much. We've pestered Abuelita for details, but the most I got from her were the words: "mecanismos estraños." Valora translated that to: "strange mechanisms."

When I asked Abuelita for more, the older woman brushed me away.

"Ay, Elbert," Valora finally said. "I don't think Abuelita knows much about guns."

But I don't understand. If Valora and Mrs. Padilla have never seen a trapper, then why are they running, especially from something that might not exist anymore?

But there's the instinct, the feeling Mrs. Padilla described as the rabbit and the coyote. She calls it a pattering in her chest that won't fade. It keeps her up late at night when she's trying to rest. If it weren't for Andrés refusing to return to them, the Padilla family would be running toward Canada by now—to hide. To survive, as Valora puts it.

Instead, they must wait for the trappers to come with their curious machines. But I wonder if they're waiting for an extinct tribe of people who no longer walk this earth. Maybe it's just shadows of the imagination driving this fear in their hearts. They'll be waiting forever, wondering. And hiding.

Chapter Twenty-Four

It's still morning, and Peto and I are rolling our bikes home from a trip to town. I skid to a stop along the side of the house and unshoulder my sack of supplies. Peto follows, dropping his own sack to the ground. Just beyond the porch, I see Jorm dash past the oak tree and head our way, pumping his arms in the air.

"Elbert!" he shouts, cranking his legs faster. "Peto!"

By the time he gets to us, sweat is dripping down the front of his neck, he's gasping for breath, and his glasses fog up. Are those tears?

A shiver works its way up my back.

"What is it?" I say, holding my breath for the answer.

"It's Pops," he says. "He's hurt."

We chase him back to the house and wrench open the front door, tumbling through the entryway.

Mom's muffled voice comes through the back room. "Trinna, help Vida, please."

Peto jumps toward the other room, and I lurch into a run. But no, I'm still here. Glued to the floor. Like a coward.

Something metal crashes against the floor.

"Careful! Not my hanging basket!" Vida's voice cries from the kitchen.

Peto waddles backward into the sitting room, gripping a pair of legs. Pops's legs.

Mom carries the other half of Pops into the room. His ruddy face grimaces with each step.

"Agh!" he bellows. "Peto, don't—let go of that leg. No, that one! Ahh!"

Pops's blood-soaked leg lands on the floor.

Mom's gaze finds its way to Jorm and me. "Stay back, Jorm." She jerks her head at me. "Elbert, you take my place."

I jump to Mom's side and hook my arms under Pops. He grunts as we shift his weight.

"Follow me, boys," Mom calls ahead of us. "Elbert first."

I shuffle, back first, into the hall. Finn slips behind me and grabs the tail of my shirt, tugging me to Mom and Pops's room.

"Right here." Mom points to the bed and helps me slide Pops onto the fresh sheets.

Pops winces and howls with every shift of his weight until he's lying flat on the bed, panting. Howly must have heard her name in all that hollering. She skitters into the room and begins licking Pops' fingers. Now that Pops is in bed, I ease my way out of the bustling room. Hopefully, no one notices me sliding back toward the door.

No one does. They're all fussing over Pops. Finn is hugging Howly, Jorm is mopping the sweat off Pops's forehead, and Mom continues handing out orders. The girls enter with bowls full of steaming water. They step lightly, like acrobats on a tightrope. Peto lumbers in with a pile of clean cloths.

"Anything else?" Peto says as he flops his pile on a chair.

I don't wait for Mom's answer. I slink away, sunk in a daze. My legs choose my destination without telling the rest of me where I'm going, and I end up standing on the back lawn.

There, I find Fuzzy Lips. A rolling cart is tipped sideways with sod sprawled across the ground. I pick my way through the clumps of dirt to the horse and press my hands against his long, silky nose. I hold on until my skipping heart slows down.

"What happened, Fuzz?" I ask the horse's glittering, black eyes.

The beast knickers and puffs on my face.

"I forgive you." I swallow a lump down my throat. "We all make mistakes."

We've always been desperate for Pops. We rely on his back, his muscled arms, his sturdy legs—and his time. It's true that we have Peto. Almost as tall as Pops, almost as wide, but still as thin as a sixteen-year-old boy. He doesn't have the strength to push through Pops' daily chores. Pops was carved from stone and lit with fire. It takes decades to forge a man like him.

And now his body is lying flat on a bed.

I peer into the master bedroom and catch a glimpse of the dark purple bruises and broken skin. Old blood has dried in his hair and down the side of his face. When his eyes meet mine, his mouth hangs open. I slip away before he can say anything.

Doc Brownly shuffles in just shy of midnight with his tired gray bag and soft, low voice. Vida and Peto are inside Pops's room with Mom, leaving only to retrieve fresh linens or a pot of scalding water. I sit in the hallway with Trinna and Finn leaning against my sides. Jorm is across from me with his chin cradled in his palms and his glasses resting on his fingertips.

We stay there throughout most of the night, nodding off with our foreheads balanced on our knees. Mom comes by and scoops us up one by one. First, Trinna. Then Finn. After leading Jorm to bed, her arms squeeze my shoulders.

I peer into her glittering eyes and notice a crease in her forehead. Uncertainty still gnaws at her, just like it clings to me.

"What if we aren't strong enough without Pops?" I say, using my thumb to swipe below my eyes.

"You're right," she says. "Sometimes we aren't strong enough. You've seen families pack up and leave this town. Sometimes it's too much. Life is hard. And sometimes it gets harder."

"Pops said something like that once." I fiddle with the hem of my sleeve. "But it won't always be this hard."

I hope.

Her smile reaches her eyes. "That's right, Elby. Life comes in seasons."

This is also true. Some seasons are easy, like spring, when all we need to do is reach out and pluck fruit from the vine. Other times, it's winter when we spend our days protecting the fields from the stormy skies, and our biggest wish is for the farm to simply *survive*.

Mom tilts her head. "A lot of things are happening right now. With Pops. With you. I just want you to consider one thing. Are you going to let these things make you stronger? Allow you to *change*?"

Change. There's that word again. A lump forms in my gut, and I shudder. "Are you telling me to change, Mom? Into the firebird?"

Heat flashes through me, and I breathe, drinking in the sharp, cool night. Just the thought makes my skin burn. I know I should change and finish this curse, but just thinking about it makes my bones shake.

"I know you're afraid of what's happening to you," she says.

"Of course, Mom. I've been cursed."

She nods, but she doesn't agree. I can sense it in her sigh. "What if I told you this is not a curse?"

I glance away. I won't be able to hide the anger creeping through me. "I'd say you've never had feathers growing out of your arms."

We sit in silence for a moment as my words settle on her.

"I'd hoped Pops would..." Her voice trails off. She was probably going to say Pops had failed somehow. I'm glad she didn't. Not when he's bedridden with a bruised leg.

She pulls out a small, leather book from the folds of her apron. "We should have spoken to you sooner. Much sooner." She pauses, then adds, "I'm sorry, Elby."

I point to the book. "What is that, Mom?" I can't hide the bitter edge in my voice. A metallic taste fills my mouth.

She's still for a moment, then she holds out the booklet. "I found this today. Had to rummage through some of Pops's things, but we both agree. You need to read this. It should answer some of your questions. We've decided, we don't want to hide this anymore. It's up to you, of course, if you want to step deeper into this magic. The more you know..."

... The more this magic spark will grow. Yes, but I want to know. I'm tired of not knowing.

I reach for the booklet and open the yellowing pages to a series of dates and tightly written script. "Is this Pops's journal?"

"No," she says and smiles. "It's Grandpa's." She flips to a page dated about thirty years ago. "Start here."

Chapter Twenty-Five

~∞~

FEBRUARY 10TH, 1875

Clara made me porridge and bacon today. The boys finished their servings before I swallowed my first bite. Radcliffe started poking me for scraps. He's nearly sixteen now. His bones are growing so fast. They must be in a hurry to get somewhere. Poor boy's entire body aches every night. But life won't be as rough for him as it was for me. He's past the age to grow his spark. It makes sense. He's too sensible. Magic would not agree with him. It would only slow him down as he pursues a career in engineering next year.

Then there's Pierson. He's only thirteen years old, nearly fourteen. He loves the outdoors—hunting, fishing, anything with adventure. And every day, I sense magic growing in him. Soon his spark will start building into a flame, and that flame will grow into magic. And it will be my job to show him how to use it.

Although this magic comes with great strengths, it also comes with weaknesses. Only a wild mind can bend this magic to his will and not get burned.

If I'm being honest, I've known for a while that Pierson is my wild son.

APRIL 30TH, 1875

We were sitting beside the fire in the backyard, just Pierson and me, talking about life and the future. The glistening moon seemed to hush the night, but it failed to soften the worries on my mind. I thought to myself, taking on magic was a big responsibility, maybe more than Pierson could handle. Maybe it would be better for Pierson to be free of this complicated magic.

I'd kept quiet these past couple months, waiting to see if Pierson's spark grew, or if it would die like it did for many of the Dowden family members. As more time passed, the fire in Pierson's eyes only grew brighter, hungrier.

There was only one thing left to do—ask the same question that I asked Radcliffe when he turned fourteen. "What future do you wish for, Pierson?"

He told me something I'll never forget.

"I want a life like yours," he said. "I want a home, a family to take care of, and I want to protect others the way you protect us. With magic."

That's the first time I knew, really knew, that my sons were aware of my ability. I have been suspicious these past few years by the way they stare at me whenever I lean over a pile of wood, even when I'm holding a match. They've stopped questioning me when I circle the village during high winter to make sure everyone has fire enough to keep warm. They've stopped complaining when I leave them in the middle of the night to help our neighboring towns battle brush fires and burning buildings. They can't smell the smoke on the air like I can—no ordinary person can, but when I came home, they must have smelled it on my clothes. They must have seen the black marks on my shirt.

Pierson has probably known about my magic for a while now. I'm not sure why he said nothing to me. Out of fear? But Pierson's eyes showed curiosity and hope. Not fear. Respect. He was waiting for me to speak. And while he waited, he trusted me. I'd been carrying the burden of this trust, especially in that moment as we sat by the fire.

"I want to use fire to keep people warm," Pierson said. "I want to save people from flaming buildings. And I want to protect my family."

He wanted a life where flames melted in his grasp, never to be burned by fire again. But I had to warn him about the bitter cold. The biting wind. The burning touch of water.

Magic is not a gift. It's a trade.

"Life won't get easier, Son," I said. "When you have this ability, you'll also feel the sting of water. And a cold wind will bite like frost. It's the balance of nature. Fire is strong, but it comes with a weakness."

He still opened his palms, hoping and waiting. The fire in my gut climbed to my chest and sparked through my arms. I considered ignoring his request to become like me. But the hope in Pierson's eyes was as certain as a prayer. If I did not help him grow this magic, he would resent me for it. And I would resent myself right along with him.

I gripped his hands, and a circling wind rushed between us. A band of heat sparked between our palms. It reminded me of the day Grams passed her fire down to me. I'd been nervous and excited—and so unprepared.

It only took a handful of minutes for my magic spark to work its way to Pierson's spark. This would accelerate the magic growing in my son, but it will also cause him pain—I remember that part too. He lost control of his limbs, and his body seized and coiled. His veins glowed golden-red underneath his skin, and his hair burned a molten color. A red cloud of dust and light burst over his body. And soon, feathers sprouted through his skin, and his toes grew long and pointed. Arches of light burned underneath his shoulders—wings of fire. The winds quieted to a whisper, the feathers and wings crumbled away, and the orange glow faded from his eyes. He was normal, average, human again. All the signs of the phoenix were gone, but I knew better.

My boy had magic coursing through his veins.

MAY 29TH, 1875

Pierson is a fast learner. He rises early every morning to practice grabbing magic from a candle. He's already mastered pulling fire into his fists and throwing flames into the trough or a water bucket, whatever he can find. The sheep have finally stopped skittering away every time he comes close.

He doesn't hide what he can do. This is strange because ever since magic claimed my life, I've always had this urge to hide it from the ones around me. Maybe out of self-protection? I think it's part of the magic, a deep sense of caution that's ingrained in me—helps me survive. But Pierson will brag about his magic, and Radcliff teases him for it. He'll say things like, "How do I know you won't catch the bedsheets on fire?"

I understand his concern, as our small cottage requires our growing boys to share a bed. I've reassured Radcliffe that Pierson has good control of his magic—and so early on. He's only burned the back of one of his shirts. I used to singe the buttons off my shirts every time I pulled fire from my chest. It took a couple years to tame my fire so it didn't bite back.

I'm just glad Radcliff doesn't fear his brother. I expected him to at least be cautious, but he has known about me and my magic all this time, so I suppose this is nothing new to him.

Clara resents me for giving Pierson his spark without her. Yesterday, we had our first fight in eight years. I suspect she'll forgive me next Christmas when I buy her that loom she's been wanting.

JUNE 3RD, 1875

Today I took Pierson to the river and forced him to wade in the water for as long as he could stand. He only lasted a handful of seconds, but he'll need to learn how to fight through the pain, or this weakness will control his life.

"How long until I become a phoenix?" he said to me.

He's been asking this question almost every day now. I should have never told him how far our abilities can grow. I don't want to admit I've never reached this level myself. To become a phoenix is the pinnacle of our magic. There are many other things we can do, like control fire, create our own flame, and occasionally, when the situation is dire, manifest wings. But to become a phoenix? So few of us ever get there. We're not like the other shapeshifters. Our magic is fire, and fire burns quickly. It devours. Those of us who do risk losing ourselves to the wild reaches of our magic, by the time we make it back to our human selves— if we make it back—we always leave something behind.

When magic grows too wild, it pulls us away from our humanity—from home. That's what Grams called it. When this happens, our souls become strangers to everything we love.

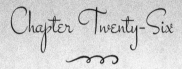

Chapter Twenty-Six

Moments before sunrise, the shadows are coldest, and every living creature has fallen asleep. Except for me. I'm still awake, thinking, while Jorm snores next to me. Two thoughts press heavily on my mind, and they are both about Grandpa's journal entries.

First, Grandpa was like me, someone who wielded fire. I barely knew the man before he died, so I should be surprised to learn this, but I'm not. Someone had to pass down the curse to Pops before it got to me. Also, Pops wanted to be cursed. *This* is a surprise. Pops has always hated the curse.

Hasn't he? I won't know unless I ask.

I groan. That means I'll have to speak with Pops. It's been hard to avoid him these past couple of days, especially when everyone is expected to tend to his wounds.

A light knock at the front door disrupts the still, quiet house. I wait, half-expecting Mom or Peto to shuffle to the entryway. I'm sure *I* didn't invite anyone over before dawn. The knock comes again. Since no one is stirring, I rise from my bed and make the trek to the entryway. When I open the door, Daichi grins back at me. He's clutching a straw hat to his chest and a bag full of tools. A breeze pushes past us, and my feathers stand on end.

"Morning, Elbert!" His gaze slides past my shoulder. "Oh, good morning, Vida."

I glance back to Vida's face glowing by candlelight. She's got her hair piled into a cushion-shaped bun, and she's wearing her Sunday best, not the simple workday dress and apron that she should be wearing.

Interesting. Looks like she's been up for hours preparing for Daichi's early arrival. Like she *knew* he was coming.

"Hi," she says, her face glowing by candlelight.

Mom shuffles next to Vida and clasps Daichi's hand in hers.

"Thank you for coming," she says.

Daichi seems unsure of what to do with this show of gratitude, and he smiles nervously at Mom. "Of course, Mrs. Dowden. That's what neighbors are for."

If I didn't already know Pops was made of magic, I know now. Not because of the fire burning inside him, but because of his leg. His broken leg has the magical power to summon half the town. First came Daichi in the dark morning hours to help prep the fields for their next planting. Another knock comes in the afternoon. I'm passing through the kitchen, so I open the door to Anne. She's clutching a basket full of cakes, fresh cloths, and a pair of working gloves. After handing the basket to Vida, she takes the gloves and follows me to the backyard where she settles into digging out weeds in the garden.

We all work late until the first signs of dusk settle in. Anne and Daichi stay with us to the end, later than necessary. By the time we set down our tools, Mom is ringing the cowbell for supper, and we drag ourselves into the house. We're greeted with platters of roasted potatoes and vegetables, chunks of bread, and the tang of freshly squeezed lemonade. Vida is glowing as she waves her oven mitts at us, pointing to the table set to accommodate the extra helpers.

We squeeze into our chairs and stools, elbow to elbow, and eat quietly, all too aware that Mom and Pops are only a few strides away, down the hall and to the left. Mom comes out midway through the meal to speak on behalf of Pops. Her tears spill over her smiling cheeks.

Daichi and Anne nod and say things like "you're welcome" and "my pleasure" until a warmth fills the room.

We stay up late trading stories and gnawing on whatever is left in the kitchen. Finally, the moon takes charge of the night, and Daichi and Anne leave with their bellies full.

And more keep coming.

On Thursday, Pastor Harvey comes for prayer. Friday, Harold's parents, Merv and Sue, knock on our door with a basket full of soap, socks, and other useful things. Even the Padillas leave a basket of medicines, after hours, of course, while everyone is in bed. One vial is labeled "for sleeping" and another labeled "for infecting." At first, the second vial confused me, but then I realized it must be for preventing infection.

I'm *pretty* sure.

Meanwhile, Pops stays in his room, even as the visitors pour in by the dozen. Is he hiding from something? Someone? Is it *me?* I don't know. Maybe it's because he's afraid to look me in the eyes. I've read Grandpa's diary. I know just how many secrets he's been keeping from us.

Leo comes at the end of the week, bearing gifts of pilling tools and useful nick knacks. He's in no hurry to get home, so we start a fire in the backyard. Jorm and Finn join us with armfuls of food—crusts of bread, cheeses, sausages, and several metal skewers.

An orange tumbles from the crack in Finn's arm.

"Are you planning on cooking that on the fire?" I stoop to grab the rolling fruit.

Finn's tubby face twitches before he answers. "I just want to see what happens."

It's not that cold outside—for the others, anyway—but we grab blankets and toss them over our shoulders. We drag over a few chairs and flip a bucket upside down for Leo's bum knee. The old man sighs and holds his pipe loosely in one hand.

"Tell us a story," Finn demands in the sweetest voice no one could deny.

"What kind?" Leo says, scratching his knee and grinning.

"Ghost story," Finn says in a low whisper, glancing back at the house. He's probably worried Mom might hear him.

"No, Leo, you don't have to do that," I say, more for Finn. Scary stories bring scary dreams, and I don't want to find my littlest brother hiking through the weeds at midnight again.

"It's okay, Elbert," Leo waves his pipe. "Ghosts are harmless."

His words are like ice pricking the back of my neck. Did Leo just say he believes in ghosts?

A swath of smoke curls past his bushy brows, and the corner of his mouth cracks open. "Ghosts are just shadows that glow."

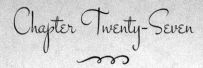

Chapter Twenty-Seven

"You believe in ghosts?" Jorm squawks.

"C'mon, Leo. You pulling our legs? What's scientific about a ghost?" I ask.

Leo winks. "Looks like I've got a story to share."

I don't like this, for Finn's sake, but I'm intrigued. We load our skewers with food and sizzle the morsels over the flames. At one point, I lean too close, and a tendril of fire jumps on me. The glowing spark crawls up my shirt, and I toss the flame back into the pit. Finn and Jorm don't bat an eye, but Leo lets out a low whistle.

"Ooh, Elbert," he says, "you're getting good at handling that fire!"

I grin. "And don't you forget it."

His eyes twinkle, and for the briefest moment, his mouth slips into a frown. He may doubt his loyalty to science right now.

We sit and chat for a while longer, scalding our tongues on our food. Finn declared his blackened orange "too mushy" and squashed it with his foot. As I pluck off the last of the roasted apple chunks from my skewer, Leo clears his throat.

"Okay," he says. "Now we're ready for a story." He scratches at his bum leg and sighs. "If you believe something is real when it's not, then it becomes dangerous. And I used to believe in something that wasn't real."

"Like ghosts?" I ask.

He grimaces. "Like ghosts."

I glance at Finn and think of Juniper. Even now, my youngest brother holds two skewers, one for him and one for his imaginary sister. I should probably send him to bed, but part of me hopes maybe Leo's story will help my little brother put Juni's ghost to rest.

Leo takes a deep breath and slumps back in his seat. "You know this already, but I had a family once, when I was living back in Missouri."

"Yes, I remember," I say. "I see your picture whenever I visit your shop."

"You do? Well, you might not know this, but it was a hard life out there in the Ozarks," he says. "The land took a beating, and so did we. Salinas is a paradise compared to my old home. I wish my wife and boy could have seen this place."

"How'd they die?" Finn says bluntly.

My mouth drops open. "Finn, you can't just *ask* him."

"It happened in winter," Leo says, undisturbed. "It was the kind of cold that stole the breath from your lungs." I hand him a hunk of toasted bread and cheese, and he nibbles at the corners. "One night, a thunderstorm rumbled in. Lightning flashed in the hills, and rain hardened into sleet. We huddled near the hearth for the night. Sometime late, after we'd all nodded off, the wood in the fire snuffed out. I kept sleeping, but not my boy. He woke up, and he must have noticed the fireplace was out because he left for more wood. My wife woke up, too, and followed him into the storm." He rubs his eyes and puffs air between his teeth. "They didn't come back."

His words sit heavily on us, and I wonder if I should say something. Finn beats me to it.

"That's not a ghost story," he says.

"Yes, you're right, boy. Not exactly. Let me get to that part." He relaxes his face, and firelight dances over his cheeks. "Remilda, that was my wife—she was strong. She grew up in the mountains. She could catch a fish with nothing but a sharp stick. Her fingers were thin and sturdy, not bothered by the damp air. She never stopped moving. Never stopped fixing broken things."

"How'd you meet?" Finn interrupts. He's leaning close to the flames, so Jorm tugs him back a couple inches.

"I left Sweden as soon as I became a man. Sailed to New York with a handful of coins. Hitched a ride south. Or—at least, that's where I thought I was going. I wanted to live in a quiet coastal town in Florida. Ended up in the harsh Ozarks of Missouri." He laughs at this part. "My English wasn't that good yet."

Jorm's eyebrows raise above his glasses.

"I know." Leo nods. "Well, I made the best of what I got. Started working on a dairy farm near the plateau—for Remilda's dad. That's where I met Remilda, among the cows. Asked her to be my wife as soon as I had enough coins to buy a plot of land."

"That's beautiful," says Finn.

"*She* was beautiful. So was our boy, Jasper. But Jasper didn't come until a few years later. We wanted a child sooner. Remilda was so impatient, hated the waiting. And we certainly waited. Ten years we tried to have a baby. After a while, Remilda lost hope, and she stopped talking about it, stopped knitting those little clothes. Until we found Jasper."

"Found?" Jorm cuts in.

The blacksmith's eyes glint with firelight. "He was just a couple years old when we found him wandering in the brush.

Didn't speak a word, didn't even know his own name, so we called him Jasper. We aren't sure what happened. Maybe his parents passed away. Maybe his family was poor and couldn't care for him, so they sent him off, hoping someone like Remilda and I would take pity on him. We took him in, clothed, bathed, and fed him. And a glow returned to Remilda. This was life for the next few years. It was beautiful and full. But as you know, it was short."

"But you said Remilda was strong. What happened?" I say.

"I'm not sure what it was—what I saw," Leo says in a deep voice.

I shudder against the cold breeze brushing the back of my neck.

Leo shudders, too. "That night, when my boy set out to find more wood, I would have kept sleeping if it weren't for the thunder. I woke up to a loud crack and a flash of light bursting through the window. And that's when I noticed they were both gone."

"And you went outside to find Remilda and Jasper?" Finn whispers, his face leaning toward the fire again.

"Yes." Leo's head droops, and his face sags, reminding me of the times Pops slumps in his chair. "I ran to the shed first, and that's where I saw it." He holds his hands up like he's measuring something. His mouth opens and closes.

"What?" I blurt. "Was it a ghost?"

"No," he whispers. "There was a beast unlike anything I'd ever seen. Well, until now."

"Was it a giant deer?" Finn asks.

"A big wolf?" Jorm says.

Moonlight glimmers in the old man's eyes. "I'm not sure what I saw in the dark. I just know this beast had wings—and it was large. Larger than an ox. It stirred up a storm. It *was* the storm. And my son lay at its feet."

"Was he okay?" Finn says before I have the chance to stop him.

Leo's mouth presses shut, and he shakes his head.

"The creature took him?" Finn says, and this time I touch his shoulder as a warning.

"It's okay," says Leo, his voice rough. "Yes, the creature scooped him up and rose above the trees. But I chased after it. Waved my shotgun and fired off a round or two." He taps his bum leg with a skewer. "Then I got zapped with lightning."

"What?" all three of us shout.

Leo laughs. "Don't you know how I got this lame leg? Run into a lightning storm. That will do it. As soon as that lightning struck me to the ground, the beast turned tail and left."

"Woah," Jorm says, gnawing on his thumbnail. "Is he still alive, then?"

Leo shakes his head. "I don't think so."

We sit quietly for a while as that last thought sinks in.

I touch Leo's shoulder. "I'm sorry."

He rests his scratchy palm on my hand. "Remilda took our son's disappearance very hard. Worse than me. She started to believe impossible things. She insisted he was still alive. I don't blame her. We never got to bury him and let him go. We planted a black walnut sapling in his memory. But then," here, Leo winces, "she starts seeing his ghost. At least, that's what she was saying."

Finn gasps and sputters on a hunk of bread. "Ghost."

Leo gives a weak smile. "But for her, he wasn't a ghost. He was still alive. She'd see him out there, roaming the hills. I never believed her. I wish—I wish I had told her just once that I believed her. Maybe—" his voice falters, "Maybe she wouldn't have left."

"She left?" Jorm says. "Did she go looking for him?"

Leo nods. "I think so. She just couldn't believe he was

gone. Just felt something deep in her soul, and she wouldn't let go. So, she just walked out one day—and that's when I started going mad."

"Did you start seeing ghosts, too?" Finn says.

Leo cracks a smile. "You're a clever one, Finn. Yes, you're right. I did see ghosts. Once."

Jorm lets out a noisy breath and whispers, "I *knew* it."

Leo continues. "I finally faced the truth: she was not coming back. Most likely, she didn't survive the search for our son. I went out to the black walnut sapling and dug two holes, one to bury a locket of Remilda's and one to bury Jasper's favorite toy as a child. While I was laying wildflowers on their graves, I saw them, staring at me in the shade of the trees—glimmering shadows, shaped like my wife and my boy."

"Woah." I shudder.

Leo shrugs. "It was all in my mind. Back then, I wanted to *believe* these were the spirits of my boy and my wife, safely on the other side of this world. But I'd lost all reason at that point —saw things that weren't there—and I welcomed this illusion. It felt so real. But deep down, I knew it wasn't. By the time night rolled in, I knew I was losing my mind, just like Remilda. I knew that if I didn't stop myself, I would start searching the hills for two ghosts that didn't exist."

"Dangerous," I murmur. "Are you listening, Finn?"

"Yes, of course." Finn huffs and crosses his arms. "But Juni isn't a ghost."

At least we agree on that. She's just his imagination.

"She doesn't glow," Finn adds.

So close.

Leo draws in another breath. "Grief is powerful. It drags you down, and it eats away the life you have. When you're sad, really sad, you'll believe things you'd never believe when you're happy."

I try to imagine Leo as a sad man. "What changed?" I say. "You don't seem sad *now*."

"A letter," Leo says.

"Was it from Remilda?" Finn asks.

Leo chuckles. "No, no. I got a letter from my sister. She doesn't live here anymore, so I don't think you ever met her. She was here back before everyone was farming sugar beets. She reached out to me, despite being on opposite ends of the country. It's like she sensed I was going mad with grief. She said her god whispered one night, warning about my troubles. She told me to come to California. Said there was a bed waiting for me." His eyes sparkle. "If I were a religious man, I'd thank her god."

"Really?" I ask, surprised.

A smile bends his mustache. "Right after I curse the devil —that winged beast—for taking my family."

We laugh at that last comment. I'm not sure if we were supposed to, but Leo doesn't seem to mind.

"So, then you came here," Finn concludes for him.

"That's right. I packed my things and came to Salinas. And survived my grief."

"How are you doing now?" I say.

He taps his pipe against his knee and squints at the fire. "It still hurts. But I'm happy again."

"Do you still miss them? Remilda and Jasper?" Finn whispers.

Leo nods. "All the time."

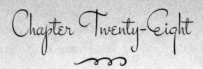

Chapter Twenty-Eight

Mom opens the door to the back porch and hollers for us to come inside, so Leo tips his hat and stomps down the embers of the fire. I'm expecting him to go on home, but he doesn't. Instead, he asks for Pops.

I want to hide behind the doorway so I can listen to their conversation, but Peto or Vida would definitely catch me. Or Mom. I linger in the kitchen, listening. Maybe if I listen hard enough, I will catch something.

"What're you doing?" A tired, rumbly voice makes me jump.

I flip and face Peto. He's got a wool blanket draped over one arm and a frown on his face.

"Shh," I say and close my eyes. "I'm listening to Pops and Leo."

"Can you hear them?"

I hold up a hand of silence, but with Peto's breathing, the creaking walls, my heartbeat, I can't catch anything past this room.

"Why don't you just talk to him, Elby?"

Talk to Pops? The liar? "No, thank you," I say.

Peto shrugs and lumbers down the hall. In the shadows, he looks like a swaggering pirate, and it annoys me.

He *is* right. I should talk to him, but I *really* don't want to.

I wait a few more minutes until the door to my parents' room opens, and someone strides softly through the hall. Most likely Leo. Or maybe not. I'd expect the steady dragging of a bum leg.

"Leo, you there?" I stir to my feet.

The old man pauses near a clump of burning candles by the entrance. He's quiet at first, then he says. "Yessir. You caught me."

I walk over, trying to read his face in the dim light. "How's your leg?"

He breaks into a smile. "Ah, boy, I forgot to show you." He pulls up the hem of his pant leg and reveals a contraption made of metal and leather that fits along his calf, just below the knee.

"How'd you get this?" I tap one of the metal knobs and notice a soft whirring sound.

"Made it myself." He beams. "Saw it in a magazine. *Inventors of the 20th Century.* Thought I could do the same. Now I glide when I walk, smoother than butter on a biscuit."

I shake my head in disbelief. "Amazing." I remember his binoculars, another impressive invention. "Have you seen anything interesting with your binoculars?"

He shifts nervously. "Yes."

"Well?"

"Saw a gator this time. Huge one. Large as a boat. Saw the wolf again a couple days back, but she ran so fast, couldn't keep her in my sights."

"And you saw that creature in the Ozarks. Are you ready to believe in magic yet?" I smirk.

"Ah, you know I'm too sensible for that. There are

168

perfectly reasonable explanations for these creatures. But have you seen any of them roaming your property? Are they bothering you?"

"No." I shake my head quickly. Probably too quickly.

He nods slowly, probably unsure if he believes me. "Okay, then. Well, let me know, Son. We all need to take care of each other."

His voice is thick with a warning, his eyes tight and wide. Is that worry or distrust? "Everything okay, Leo?"

"I just want to make sure you're being safe. We don't know what these creatures can do."

Does he know something? Are people talking about my trips to the river? I wouldn't be surprised if Jorm blabbered. He's not one for keeping secrets.

"I'll be fine. I'm part beast, you know." I laugh nervously.

"That's true." His brows sag, but his face crinkles into a smile.

"What are you thinking about?" I say, interrupting the thoughts dancing across his eyes.

"I was thinking about your Pops. He misses you."

"Yeah, I know."

After Leo mounts his horse and trots off, I shuffle down the hallway and creak open the door to my parents' room. The smell of alcohol and wet rags sting my nose. Pops has his leg resting on a pile of books topped with a cushion. When he recognizes me in the glow of the kerosene lamp, his jaw drops. He stays silent and stiff, as if afraid he'll scare me away.

"Hi, Pops." I have no clever greeting to share. If I say too much, I'd tell him exactly what's on my mind—that I'm disappointed with how many things he's been hiding. Especially after reading that journal.

"Hi, Son," he says. His voice is low and scratchy, like he's been crying.

"Does it hurt?" I point to his injuries.

He heaves a low, pitiful sigh. "Depends. Will I get more sympathy if it does?"

I try not to smile.

"If I say I'm near the brink of death, will you promise to steal one of Vida's cakes? I know she's hiding them behind the sack of flour in the kitchen."

A grunt escapes my lips. "I don't know."

"I'll share."

That's a lie. He never shares.

I leave the room to grab the cake. When I return, he breaks a hunk off for me.

So he wasn't lying after all.

I sink my teeth into the soft, yellow treat. The sweet honey glaze soothes my tongue.

"Like biting into paradise," he murmurs. And for a moment, I feel normal again.

"What did Leo say?" I break the silence.

He puffs air like Fuzzy Lips and chuckles. "Told me about his ghosts."

"Sounds about right."

His tired eyes glisten. "I'm sorry, Son. I should've talked to you sooner about everything. Obviously, hiding this did not help you. I thought I was protecting you. But it's clear, magic does what it wants. You must be different from Peto and Vida. I wish I'd known that."

I swallow and nod. I'm not ready to forgive him out loud, but there's a loosening in my chest. "I've been reading Grandpa's diary," I say. "You wanted the curse. Why?"

He slouches in his seat. "It wasn't a curse. More like I didn't think of it like that. Not back then."

"What about now?"

He breathes loudly before he answers. "It's more of a burden. I have this overwhelming urge to hide it from others."

"I feel that, too." I rub the feathers on my arm and realize something. "I haven't felt the urge to hide in a while, though. Maybe because I can't hide anymore."

But I remember the diary entry. Pops wasn't always this way. He was proud of his magic. Well, at first.

"What changed?" I ask. "Grandpa says in the journal you weren't afraid to have magic. You didn't want to hide." I can guess why, but I want him to say it. I want the mystery gone.

He's slow to answer. He's always so slow, and I don't have the patience to wait.

"C'mon Pops. Why did my magic keep growing? Grandpa helped yours get stronger, but that's what you wanted. You said if I don't want this, it will go away." I shut my eyes. "It's not going away."

Pops rubs his eyes and stares at the corner of the room. "I don't know."

"You don't know? Seriously?" I clench my fists and tuck my arms against my chest.

"I told you, Son. I was trying to protect you. But magic does what it wants."

"Maybe it would have been different if you didn't keep everything a secret. I could have done something. Protected myself. But you hid your magic away, even from us, for so long."

Pops is quiet. Too quiet. "I don't know how to say it." His head droops over his chest. He looks ready to break into sobs, but he doesn't. Instead, he goes silent.

"Were you hiding because of Juni?" I whisper, my heart cracking.

He grimaces and nods. A sadness weighs him down, and I realize Pops carries a pain deeper than mine, but somewhere along the way, it has hooked its nails into my heart. As Pops grieves for Juniper, I grieve for Pops.

As much as I miss Juniper, love, and cherish her memory, my deepest pain comes from watching Pops fade and crumple. Something about the way he breaks apart scares me, and his hurt becomes my hurt. We all grieve for Juniper, but Pops is the one holding onto her ghost—not like Finn, who has turned her into a friend. Pops holds onto the pain of Juniper —and I'm holding onto Pops.

I need to let go. Of something. I don't know how or what exactly, but whatever this is... it's sinking me into the ground. I don't think Juniper would want this. She wouldn't want to be the reason any of us fall apart.

I get an idea and leave the room. When I return, I've got Grandpa's journal and a fountain pen. I flip to a blank page near the back.

"Write it down, Pops. Even the hard parts."

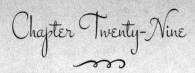

Chapter Twenty-Nine

The next evening, near the end of the workday, Peto calls for us to put down our pilling tools. I race back inside to change into a fresh shirt—the blue one. I want to show off my eyes against this blue fabric because tonight is an important night. Tonight, the magic that has been growing inside Valora will spark into something more. I still don't understand why she welcomes this curse into her life, but she asked me to be there when she sparks, so I will be there.

I stroll toward the kitchen. Maybe I'll grab a snack before I head to the river. I'm rounding the corner to the entryway when I sense a presence in the room. I halt and sink back into the hallway.

Who's here?

The rumble of a stranger's voice fills the entryway. He sounds familiar, but I'm not sure. I inch forward until I glimpse the back of a man's head. His dark gray hair is slicked sideways, and a leather strap hangs on his neck. My heart takes a tumble, and I jump back.

Mr. Halifax is in my house?

I peek again, keeping hidden in the hallway. This time, I

notice a pile of books resting on the side table. Mom is listening to him speak like he's simply a stranger in need of directions.

I can't believe this. What is he doing here? My heart pounds in my ears while I strain to listen in on the conversation. I thought this man was harmless, just an observer, but here he is in my *home*. I should interrupt them and demand Mr. Halifax explain himself. Why has he been watching the Padilla women?

And why did Mom let him in the house?

"Elbert? Is that you?" Mom says. She might as well have fired a gun, alerting this man to my presence.

I flinch and step forward. The man's gaze falls on me, his mustache twitching as he smiles. "Elbert." His eyes twinkle, curiously warm and inviting. "How are you?"

I step forward, or Mr. Halifax moves to me. I'm not sure how it happens, but I'm shaking this man's sweaty hands. I take deep breaths to cool down. As suspicious as he might be, he has not proven to be my enemy. Not yet.

"What are you doing here?" My voice comes out as a whisper.

His face lifts in surprise, but he reaches out and gives my lightly feathered arm a firm shake. "Good to see you again. Looks like the feathers are coming along nicely."

I shudder. Has he been watching me like some beast in the field? I want to point out his strange habit of secretly taking pictures of people, but I'm worried he'll talk about the Padilla women. Instead I stay silent and wait for someone to explain what's going on.

Mom clears her throat. "Elby, Mr. Halifax is here at your father's request."

My body temperature slowly rises as bitterness settles in. Pops asked to see this man? *Why?*

I nod at Mom, biting my tongue.

Mr. Halifax gathers up his pile of books and moves toward Pops's room. Then he pauses, leaning back on his shiny brown shoes. "Elbert, you'll want to hear this."

Curiosity wins, and I swallow a breath and follow.

"Hello, Hal," Pops says as I shuffle behind the stranger's back.

"Pierson. Good to see ya."

When did Pops start having a first-name relationship with this man?

Pops shifts in the bed and gestures for Mr. Halifax to have a seat. My father's eyes are heavy, like he knows he's about to hurt me. "It's time for me to tell you something important, Elbert."

I clench my jaw and blink, refusing to speak.

"Remember how I told you I was looking for a cure?"

A cure. What would this man know about a cure?

Pops continues. "Mr. Halifax is not just a photographer from San Francisco. He's also a researcher. He's been looking for your cure."

What?

Mr. Halifax stands, his face soft and curious. A twinkle lights his eyes. Maybe I was wrong to doubt Mr. Halifax. I've been wrong about so many things lately. Has he been searching for a cure the whole time? Maybe he didn't start his search until after I met him—after I caught Pops collecting fire by the river. That's when Pops promised to find a cure.

Mr. Halifax clears his throat. "Your father came to me after the river fire. He asked me to research your family's—erm—condition. I went to San Francisco first and searched the archives there. I read whatever mythos I could find. Went to the library every day. Learned quite a lot, in fact. Made some friends. One of them was a cat—"

Pops taps his arm, steering him back to the point.

"Right. Good. Good." He gestures to a stack of books

neatly balanced on his seat. "I read about the Chinese fenghuang, the fénix of Mexico, and the phoenix of ancient Greece. But none of these manuscripts explained why a human could become a mythological firebird."

He pauses, waiting for me to respond. I stay silent.

"Right. Good. I started exploring other myths. And that's when I got to Mexican folklore and the shapeshifters. These shapeshifters can change from human to creature. But the problem is, none of the creatures mention a phoenix. But I found something." His eyes light up like a match. He cracks open one of the books on his seat and tugs out several newspaper clippings. "I started researching the local news columns, and then I found, well, I believe you saw the clippings yourself that day you came to my apartment."

"What?" Pops grunts. "He went to your apartment?"

Mr. Halifax nods on my behalf. "Yes, he did. Walked right into my room. Snooped through my things. Even dropped a spark of fire."

Pops raises an eyebrow, but I ignore him. "Go on," I say to Mr. Halifax. "Finish your story."

"Right. Good," Mr. Halifax continues. "As you know, there are others. The stag. The crocodile. And there's the wolf. Still, they're not exactly like you. Their powers come from the earth. But you are different, Elbert." He waits for me to meet his gaze. "Your magic powers come from fire."

Yes, I know. I know all of this. But I act dumb and nod my head and murmur surprise.

"I thought about it," he continues, "and I remembered that I'm not searching simply to understand you. It's to *cure* you."

Nerves fire through me as I latch onto my deepest desire to be normal—back to my old self. "Did you find a cure?"

His mustache bends with his grin. "Yes." He picks through his pile of books until he finds a small, dog-eared booklet with a dusty red cover. He holds it up and reads the title. "*La Cura: A Guide to Medicines and Magic.* This is it, Elbert."

He hands the book to me. It's heavier than I expect. "What am I supposed to do with this?"

Mr. Halifax laughs. "Oh, Gee. Right. Right. I'm trying to tell you this is the book that led me to your cure."

"Cure?" My voice dwindles to a whisper.

"Yes. But it's nothing I can do for you. You'll need to ask your friends."

My breath catches in my throat. Does he know I've been visiting the Padillas? Did Pops tell him I've been going off to the river?

"What do you mean? Are you talking about—" I stop short of saying their names. The Padillas are in hiding. If this man knows something, I shouldn't tell him *more* things. I clear my throat. "Sorry, I'm not sure what you're talking about."

"Oh?" His face pinches into a frown. Even though I'm a terrible liar, he seems to believe me. "I'm talking about the shapeshifters living upriver," he says.

I glance at Pops. Did he know about the Padilla family? He doesn't seem surprised.

"Don't you see, Elbert?" Excitement lights the stranger's eyes. "They aren't just shapeshifters. I believe, well, I'm *fairly* certain that they know La Cura. Magic that cures." He points to the faded burn marks on my arms. "They are medicine women with a grasp on magic. They can break your curse."

Heat blossoms in my chest. I'm not sure if I'm relieved to finally have information about a cure, or if this is anger growing inside me. The Padillas can cure me? But they never said anything.

Pops lands a hand on Mr. Halifax's arm and leans toward me. "I know it's a lot, but remember, I hired this man to find a cure. What I know, *he* knows. And I know a lot. I know you fell in the river at the church picnic, but you seemed fine when we found you. That water should have burned you, crippled you. Maybe it did. Someone healed you, didn't they?"

"That's not true, Pops," I growl, but I have no handy excuse to throw off suspicion.

Mr. Halifax eyes us timidly, like he's afraid we'll break into a fistfight. His next words are quiet and careful. "This is good news, Elbert. We found someone who can show you a cure."

I should be excited. A cure. It's all I've wanted these past couple of months. But right now, I'm embarrassed. I've been so careless. If Mr. Halifax could track my whereabouts, how many others saw me come and go? How many others know the true identity of the shapeshifting women?

I stare down the man who has spent weeks searching for a way to help me heal. Even as he stares with sorrow in his eyes, bitterness burns my throat. I don't care if he's trying to help. I didn't ask for it. Now he knows intimate details about my friends. Details that could put them in danger if the wrong person hears it.

Anger weighs on me, so I speak out loud. "If you hurt them, Mr. Halifax, I will hurt you back."

Chapter Thirty

I wait until dark before sneaking out the back door. Grabbing one of the bikes, I pedal through the dirt and clumps of grass, heading for the river. Tonight, Valora grows her spark, and I don't want to miss this life-changing event for her, but I do have questions. I have lots of questions, hard ones, too. And I will get my cure.

The winking stars speckle the night, and I arrive at the women's hut, still seething from my conversation with Halifax. And now resentment is rustling to the surface. Did they know? Did they have a cure for me all this time and just never tell me?

I dismount and take in the quiet surroundings. Except for a dirt bunny skittering across the moonlit grounds, everything is still. Normally, I'd assume the women were sleeping, but I know better. None of them will be sleeping at this hour, especially not on such an important night.

I pick my way through the shadows and head for the riverbed. As I move closer, I spot three figures standing where the river should be. I recognize Valora. She's between her mother and grandmother.

Abuelita notices me first and waves.

"Elberto!" she says. "Ven acá!"

I know those words. *Come here!*

I slide down the embankment and step onto the wrinkled clay, still faintly moist. Magic buzzes underneath my feet.

Mrs. Padilla walks over and grips my shoulders. "I'm glad you came." Shadows cover up her grin, but there's a warmth to her touch. It seeps into my chest and hushes my anger. Now is not the time for questions. I'll save them for after Valora's sparking ceremony, or whatever these women are calling this event.

Abuelita tucks a couple of fingers in my hand and squeezes, and I move to greet Valora. That's when my jaw pops open.

She's wearing a traditional Mexican dress, white and ruffled in the pale moonlight. Her braided hair is coiled neatly on top of her head. Starlight illuminates a single white flower wedged behind her ear. She stands gracefully as I try not to stare longer than I already have.

"You're beautiful," I whisper.

Did I just say that out loud?

A husky laugh bubbles up in Abuelita, and Mrs. Padilla frowns.

"You're late," Valora smirks with a glint in her eyes.

My tongue sticks to the roof of my mouth as all I can do is nod. I feel heavy, like a stone weighs me down, and I sink to a sad place in my heart, and then somewhere deeper than that—to bitterness. Toward myself. Someone beautiful and strong like Valora doesn't need compliments from a clumsy chicken boy with toes the size of carrots.

"It's time for your blessing, Valora," Mrs. Padilla says, tugging back a strand of Valora's hair. "Are you ready?"

Valora tightens her lips, and something settles in her eyes.

It's not sadness or fear—nothing bad like that. What is the word?

Hope. It's aching and unsatisfying because it means waiting for something good to happen. The hope on Valora's face settles the sourness in me, and for the first time since the curse, I question my anger.

Valora waits, unwavering, for the spark that will change her life. A moment that would fill me with fear. But the way these women hold each other and speak their words, the hope is plain on their faces.

And I want what they have.

Abuelita speaks something in Spanish and nudges me backward until my heels reach the shoreline.

Mrs. Padilla translates. "You should stand back, Elbert. Just in case."

Abuelita shuffles to Valora's side, and both mother and grandmother put a hand on the girl's head and the other on her shoulder. All three of them close their eyes.

A swift wind whips into the hollow riverbed, and with it, a hazy green glow. Concentrated bubbles of light burst from Mrs. Padilla and Abuelita's palms. The light sinks into Valora's head and shoulders and glows under the surface of her skin. She gasps, and her eyes fling open, lit with green fire.

More winds crash into us, and I'm knocked to the ground. I roll to my knees and squint past the swirling haze of magic. Valora is on her back now with a blanket of green light covering her body. She still grips the hands of her mother and Abuelita. Then slowly, the wind eases to a soft breath, and the glow shimmering over Valora fades.

Abuelita shrieks and claps her hands while Valora wobbles to her feet. Mrs. Padilla tugs her daughter into a firm embrace.

"Ven acá!" Abuelita calls to me, but I can't move. I'm lost in this dream, a beautiful, warm moment where magic brings... joy.

Abuelita runs to me, gripping my arm and pulling me into their circle. Tears sparkle in her eyes. She laughs her husky laugh and sways back and forth. "Dance!" The word is clear on her tongue. "Dance with us, Elbert!" she giggles. She must see the shock on my face.

Did she learn these words for this specific moment? So, she could speak to me without translation? The gesture crumbles my heart. So much kindness and acceptance. Warmth oozes through me as the three women dance circles in the mud.

Budding tears smear my eyesight. I can't stop them from tumbling down my face. I can't help but laugh. Or is this a sob?

Valora circles me, her braid hanging loose.

At some point, when I'm gasping for breath but not ready to stop this dance, I notice an odd-shaped tree bending in the breeze.

But that's not a tree.

"Andrés?" I say, stuttering to a stop.

The women slow their steps. The stag, black against the starlight, peers at us with his emerald eyes. One moment he's there, hovering over us, and the next moment he's gone, a glistening moon in his wake.

"Are you okay?" I ask Valora. We're lounging at the edge of the dry riverbed. Abuelita and Mrs. Padilla have already retired to the hut for a night's rest, but Valora is wide awake, jittering with energy.

"I'm good. I'm great. Feels like I just filled a hole inside me." She sucks in a breath.

"Can you do anything with your magic yet?"

She traces a finger across the dirt and a green glow trails

behind. A patch of grass stretches toward her hand. "Ooh!" she squeals. "Look at that."

She's so excited and carefree. Not sure why, but the happiness on her face makes my stomach churn.

"I can't wait until I learn how to shift," she says, her eyes sparkling.

That explains my twisting stomach. She wants to shift like it's a good thing. Like this is how it should be.

I swallow down a bitter taste on my tongue. "Do you get to choose which animal you shift into?"

She hesitates. "Yes, but Mom and Abuelita say a deer is best. Andrés might trust me more if I'm a deer. And I might be able to communicate with him."

She sounds wistful, like this is not really what she wants.

"Do you get to have antlers like Andrés?" I don't know of any female deer species with antlers, but if she doesn't get to have antlers—that would be disappointing.

"Oh." She rubs her chin as she ponders. "I'll have to ask Abuelita about that."

After sitting in silence for a good minute, I change the subject. "Happy birthday, by the way."

I was going to bring her one of Vida's cakes—stolen, of course, because I know nothing about baking, but I'd been carrying around anger all evening. I'd completely forgotten to grab one by the time I rushed out of the house.

"Did you bring me something?" She grins and leans close. The scent of ginger tickles my nose.

I sigh and whisper a laugh. I'm too embarrassed to answer her question, but then I remember I've got something lodged in my front pocket. I fumble for the booklet and hand it to her.

"*La Cura: A Guide to Medicines and Magic*," she reads aloud. She cracks open the spine. "Hmm. This one's in English."

She doesn't sound impressed.

"Do you have one of these already?"

She flips to a page about relieving earaches. "Abuelita has a book like this, but it's in Spanish."

So, Mr. Halifax was right. These women are not just shapeshifters. They know La Cura. Healing magic. Excitement and cold betrayal wrestle in my stomach. "Can you please tell me the truth? The complete truth?"

"Yes, of course, Elbert." Her face is softer than usual, and there's something about the way she says my name, like she's calling me "friend."

"Do Abuelita and Mrs. Padilla use La Cura?"

She blinks, clearly not expecting this question. "Yes, of course. They practice La Cura all the time. That's how we healed your burns so quickly. And my burns." She holds up her lightly scarred arms. "It's just remedies mixed with magic."

I prepare to ask my next question, but a swell of anger makes me pause. I don't like bringing things up with bitterness in my heart, but I have to know. I'm here to find a cure. And these women may have been hiding it from me.

"Is it true that..." A grip of emotion tightens my chest. "Your mother and Abuelita are able to *cure* me?"

I sound upset, even to my own ears. She looks down at a lock of her hair. A look of disappointment crosses her face.

"I wondered..." she whispers. "You really hate your magic?"

I don't want to admit this out loud, but she's right. "It wouldn't be so bad if I didn't look like a giant chicken."

She doesn't laugh at my joke. Maybe she knows I'm not really joking. "We cannot cure you," she says.

"Of course you can. La Cura. It means 'The Cure.' Stop lying to me."

She doesn't react to my anger. Just looks sorry for me. This is worse than taking offense. It means she really won't help me.

Something inside me breaks, and the hope I have left crumbles to ash. I'm going to be stuck like this forever. The thought—the truth—overwhelms me, and I break into sobs.

Valora is patient, giving me space for my grief. And when I wrangle the sobs back down my throat, she presses her hand against my shoulder. Her touch is different. Warmer, stronger, like she's pouring strength into my bones.

"We can't cure you—because you aren't sick."

Not sick? The hollow truth presents itself before me. "How can you be sure? Can't you at least try?"

"There's nothing wrong with you, Elby. Magic is not a disease."

I know she's telling the truth. Deep down, the magic echoing in my bones agrees with her. So, this is who I am? Who I'm changing to become. And I can't stop it?

I face the glistening moon, and my thoughts wander back to the moment Valora sparked. There was so much hope, so much love, warmth, and joy.

Why can't I feel that way about my own magic?

"What did your mom say to you before you sparked?" My gaze lingers on the bridge of her nose for too long, so I glance back at the moon.

"She asked if I was ready for my blessing."

Blessing. That's what her family calls this.

I breathe deeply and exhale. For these women, a life of magic doesn't mean losing a piece of themselves. For them, magic is not a trade. It's a blessing.

"What is it, Elbert?" Valora is leaning over me now, her eyebrows bunched together.

"I'm thinking."

I remember the crumpling sadness that weighs down Pops, and then there's Valora, so full of light and lifting joy.

That's what I want. I want that joy.

"I want to believe," I say. "I want to *trust* in my magic the way you do."

A grin tugs at the corner of her mouth. "Are you ready to call your curse what it really is?"

Even though so much of me still disagrees, I test the word, breathing it out loud. "Blessing."

A weight slides off my chest. And for the first time in a long time, the sourness in my gut fades.

We spend a few more quiet moments admiring the night sky before returning to the hut. I stand at the doorstep, strangely conscious of where to put my hands. Finally, I settle for my pockets. Valora tugs at the flower behind her ear.

It's time to say goodnight, but I'm not sure how to end our conversation. A pat on the shoulder is too impersonal, a hug too bold. I settle for squeezing her hand. She squeezes back, sucking the air from my lungs.

She leans closer, inspecting me. "You okay?"

Her cheek is so close to mine, I catch scents of lemon, moist clay, and lingering ginger. My face heats like a kerosene lamp, and my arms go limp.

"Yes," my voice squeaks at the end.

"Ay dios. Quiere besarme." She smirks like she just dug up a secret. "Not today. Maybe someday."

"Is that a promise?" I ask.

She stiffens and pulls back, her eyes dancing across my face. "You understood that?"

A cold panic shoots me in the gut. Did I scare her? My Spanish has improved a lot these past few weeks. Yes. I understood exactly what she said. But does she *want* me to understand?

"Yes. You said I want to hug you." It's a lie. Sounds like a probable mistake. "Besarme" does have the word "arm" in it.

Her face relaxes. A glint lights her eyes, and she plucks the flower from her hair and cups it in her hands. A green glow bubbles in her palms. When the light fades, she holds the flower—now glistening softly—out to me. "Here, Pollo."

"What's this for?" I take the flower. It's warm to the touch, like sun-soaked grass.

"It's for you, Elbert."

There's something about the way she says my actual name, like she's calling me a man, and not the boy she once whacked with a shovel.

"Thank you," I murmur. I'm not sure what else to say as fire dances in my chest.

"I covered it with magic, the kind that keeps it alive," she says.

"Thank you," I say again. I can't think of bigger words right now.

We stand quietly for a bit. The silence is unbearable.

"OK, well, goodbye," I say.

"Wait," she says, then pauses. "I hope you know... you're not a chicken."

I smile. "Yes, I know. Pollo is a nickname. I don't mind nicknames, it's okay."

"No, Elbert." She grips my arm lightly, grazing my violet-orange feathers. She doesn't shrink back. "You're not a chicken. You are a *phoenix*."

Her words sink deep, down to my bubbling shame. It covers me like a blanket and keeps me warm. Something powerful fills the ache in my heart. In a way, I'd forgotten this simple fact.

I am a phoenix.

Chapter Thirty-One

I drift on a cloud that night as I bike home. I replay everything in my head—Valora's beaming face as magic grew inside her, Abuelita's arms swaying in the air as she dances circles around me, Mrs. Padilla trying not to cry. That awkward pause before Valora went into the hut. *Quiere besarme.* She thought I wanted to kiss her. I don't know if that's true. I hadn't been thinking about that.

Now I'm thinking about it.

And then there's her gift—the flower that never dies. It sits in my shirt pocket, keeping me warm, like those last words she spoke.

You are a phoenix.

I've been calling myself a chicken all this time. It's hard to believe someone as awkward and strange as me could be something so mystical and powerful as a phoenix.

But with that power comes danger. My hands burned Valora's skin. I could have done worse, irreparable harm, yet somehow, she forgives me. She *trusts* me. How can she trust me when I don't even trust myself?

My thoughts are still buzzing when I get to the house.

Everything is dark, so I sneak into the back door and set up a bed of blankets by the dying hearth. I don't want to wake up Jorm, or anyone, really. I want to enjoy remembering this day in peace. This was a hard day. Hard at first, but in the end, something good came from it. This is the first time the curse didn't feel quite so much like a curse.

I'm not sure what it's called, but a good feeling is stirring in my chest. It keeps me warm even when the outside is so cold. It's stronger than fire.

This is more than magic. This must be hope.

A howl crashes into my dreams and yanks me awake. I sit upright in my bed, surrounded by silence.

Was that howl part of my dream, or was that real?

Another strangled yelp reaches my ears. Sounds like it's coming from the river. I leap to my feet and trip over Howly on my way to the back door. Stepping onto the porch, I wobble to my knees as a powerful gust of wind tips me off balance. I lean into the stinging breeze and search the fields.

The sky is black as soot, but even in the waning starlight, I glimpse a boy slinking between rows of sugar beets.

That's *Harold*.

He's running toward the howl with a pitchfork in one hand.

I follow at a distance as Harold runs to the spot on the river where a rope swing sways loose in the breeze. I pass a few more clumps of evergreens and pause, peering past the arms of an oak tree. Ragged breaths and the jingling of chains reach my ears, and I come to Harold lifting his pitchfork, aiming for something. I peer past the shadows and spot a giant wolf— Mrs. Padilla.

"Stop!" I leap toward Harold and knock him sideways,

but I'm too late. His pitchfork is already lodged in Mrs. Padilla's foot.

Harold rolls to his knees. His squinty eyes widen. "Elbert? What are you doing?"

Mrs. Padilla is whimpering and gnawing at a giant steel trap clamped around her front paw. And now there's the pitchfork stuck in her leg.

So, it was Harold all this time, setting traps. And now he's gotten wise and built a trap big enough to catch a giant wolf.

"Mrs. Padilla!" I run over to inspect the trap's metal teeth clamped around her fur. She sniffs the top of my head as I grip the handle of the pitchfork. That's when I realize the pitchfork is not in her leg but jammed between the jaws of the trap. "Harold, were you trying to—"

"Help her, yes," Harold says.

"Why are you helping?" I stare him square in the face.

He holds my gaze. "I heard her howling."

I'm not convinced. When has he ever wanted to help any of *us*?

"I know, Elbert." His eyes drop to the ground. "I wasn't kind to you. I was afraid of you and *them*. But when that stag —when that boy—healed Chewbie."

Mrs. Padilla leans close to Harold. He flinches and steps back a step or two.

"Does she understand me?" he whispers, glancing over at me.

"I don't know," I say. I'd never really thought of that.

The wolf leans closer to Harold and sniffs his chest. He holds up his hands in surrender while the wolf inspects him. Seemingly satisfied, she huffs and resumes gnawing on the trap. When that fails, she yanks her paw and howls in pain, thrashing and pulling the chains taut.

"Easy there, ma'am," he calls. "You'll only make things worse."

He's right. The steel jaws are as wide as a bike tire and jagged. Any struggle would only wound her leg more. Mrs. Padilla whimpers, but she stops yanking at the chains.

"I've never seen a trap this *big*," Harold says. "These levers are huge. We'll need a lot of force."

He rests the top of his boot on one of the levers and gestures me over. I hesitate, peering into my former friend's eyes. Can I trust him? Harold waits patiently, almost like he knows I'm doubting. He doesn't have that same fear as before. He's not staring at me like I'm some monster, and even now when I'm as feathery as ever.

I press my foot against the other lever and nod. Harold smiles slightly and returns my nod. So, that's it. We are as we should be. Friends again.

I lean on the lever with my full weight, but it doesn't budge. Just as I start to lean harder, something metal pokes my back. Harold peers over my shoulder and pales.

I want to flip around and face this person like a man. No doubt, this person is a trapper. But whatever is pressed against my spine could be a gun, so I drag my foot off the lever and wait for the stranger to speak.

"That's good, Elbert."

I choke on a gasp. That grizzled voice.

"Leo?" A chill builds in my throat.

I turn and gawk at my friend's haggard face. He stands, slumped forward in a bulky overcoat, an odd choice of clothing for this warm time of year. Then he grimaces and his rifle dips to the ground.

But that's not a rifle. It's a much heftier weapon made of a sleeker, sharper material. A white fire glints between gaps in the design, and a soft whirring ticks softly, like the innards of a clock.

"What are you doing?" I try to keep calm, blinking back

anger and surprise. I notice a thick leather strap pinching his throat. Something is hanging off the back of his neck.

"These creatures are dangerous, Elby. You know that. One of them took my boy." His voice is thin and raspy. Sweat glistens on his forehead. "I need to stop this one from hurting someone else."

Harold peers around Mrs. Padilla's massive hindquarters.

"Harold." Leo's mouth gapes. "You're here, too?" He hesitates, looking back and forth between Harold and me. My guess is he wasn't planning on fighting against friends today.

Mrs. Padilla growls so low, the ground rumbles underfoot. Leo slides his metal leg back and yanks his gun up to her eyes. I notice his sword dangling at his side.

"Think about what you're doing, Leo," I say, inching toward him. I count the number of steps I need to reach the barrel of his strange rifle mechanism.

"Shush, Elbert. This is between me and the beast," Leo barks, but there's pain in his eyes. His arms quiver as he lifts the muzzle.

Five steps. That's all I need.

"Don't do it," Harold whispers. "You don't know what you're—"

I leap for Leo's elbows and push his arms above his head. The snout of the weapon waves, aiming at the sky. I knock it to the ground.

"Stop!" I cry. "She's my friend."

Leo frowns. "Your friend?"

"She isn't dangerous. Leave her alone."

He stares at me like I'm a stranger. "What? Are you crazy? I know you think you're like them, but you're not a beast, Elby. Sure, you've got some feathers growing, but you're a boy. A good boy."

I grip his shoulders and peer into his sky-blue eyes. "Leo, please. You don't know what you're doing."

He stares back for a minute, studying me, no doubt testing the logic of my words. Then the sound of metal grinding through weeds rolls toward us.

What is that? *Who* is that?

Leo flicks his gaze behind my shoulder.

I whip around and face a man and woman riding toward us on what look like bicycles, but instead of canvas-wrapped wheels, metal tubes crunch through the dirt, and a column of steam puffs out the back, pushing them forward. When they reach us, the man and woman dismount from their contraptions, and a young girl pops out from behind the woman's back.

Wait. I know these people. That woman, that man, and the girl with the unblinking eyes. The red-haired folk from Leo's shop. They're a family of trappers? But the way Leo spoke to them at the shop—it was like they'd been old friends, not strangers from out of town. And here they stand, all of them in bulky overcoats.

"You caught one." the man strides up to Leo, ignoring Harold and me—and the giant beast.

The man's words sink in. This is Leo's trap? Of course, it is. And how does he know *these* people?

"Are these boys helping, too?" The woman jabs a thumb my way. "Lord knows, we could use them. You said there's three of these beasties, right?"

Harold cocks his head and scoffs, clearly offended. "We are not helping."

Now would be the time to stay silent about our true feelings. Apparently, Harold does not know this rule.

"You recruited trappers?" I say to Leo, straining to keep my voice neutral while trying to distract everyone from Harold. I might be part firebird, but I doubt I can fight off this many trappers all by myself. Better keep quiet about the fact I've befriended these "beasties."

"You could take 'em, Elby," Harold mumbles.

I hope no one heard that.

The woman grinds the metal tips of her gloves together and grins. "Takes a trapper to know a trapper. We heard this town was crawling with beasties. Of course, we were hired by someone who has a mark on one. Ain't worth fighting magical critters for free." She glances at me, more carefully this time, and flinches. "Ah. You're—you're that boy at the shop. The one with the feathers on his face."

"I didn't put a mark on this one," Leo growls, angling between me and the woman. "Just the wolf, the crocodile, and the stag. He's just a harmless half-beastie, anyway."

As soon as the words dropped from Leo's mouth, my heart patters like a spooked rabbit. Leo isn't just a trapper recruiting more trappers. He's put a mark on the entire Padilla family! The full weight of my grizzled friend's betrayal sinks into my stomach.

Mrs. Padilla growls and bares her teeth, but none of the trappers flinch. They must know, like Harold knew, the more she struggles, the more she'll mangle her leg.

I have to think of a lie. A good one.

"C'mon, Elbert. Throw magic at 'em." Harold whips his pitchfork to attack position.

The young girl snickers behind her father's back. A large club balances in her palm. With every shift of her hand, the weapon whirs and clicks, just like Leo's gun.

Harold shrinks a little, but he grits his teeth and squints, waiting for the girl to make the first move. "Go on, Elbert. Show them what you're made of."

Without my consent, a fire starts rumbling in my chest. The skin behind my ears burns. I can't lose control of myself.

Not right now.

A whirring sound ticks by my ear. I spin around, and sure enough, Leo has grabbed his weapon from the ground. He's aiming at me again, an unexpected sadness weighing down his eyes. Would he shoot? Really? The male trapper's eyes flash like a blade, and he reaches behind his neck to slide a mask over his face—unlike any I have ever seen—with tubing and shaded windows over the eyes.

He reaches inside his over-sized coat. I catch a glimpse of a metal vest and hidden gadgets—mechanisms hidden from the ordinary world. Before he can pull out a weapon, before Leo can pull the trigger, before the woman has enough sense to knock me to the ground, I gather fire in my fists and step backward, away from Leo's gun and the masked family. Someone is screaming. I think it's me.

"No!" I shout, and hold out an armful of fire. "Leave us alone."

A shadow moves between the gray trees, and a touch of dawn catches a pair of eyes, two emerald sparks. It's Valora. She's screeching, her green eyes bright like fire. She tumbles to the wolf who is now howling and thrashing and swiping at the trappers.

"Mamá!" She cries. Fear sinks into her face.

I know this fear because I feel it too, crawling up the back of my neck.

"Stay back." I wave my armful of fire, right before a blinding light knocks me to the ground.

Chapter Thirty-Two

Smoke curls past my face and seeps into my ears. A thick humming needles my brain. I push the heels of my hands against my eyes and bury my head into my knees. Time passes. Forward or backward? I'm not sure. I wait for the hurricane swirling around me to putter out. But it doesn't. It never will, so I force my eyes open and face the smoke and something else crackling off to the side, orange flames.

Did I start that fire?

Rumbling snarls and human cries reach my ears. I twist in the dirt and catch a glimpse of a massive shadow snapping at a metal-covered limb.

No. Not a limb, a weapon. A gun the size of a mid-sized cannon.

"Abuelita!"

Valora's voice pulls me to my feet. She scrambles onto the back of the shadow shaped like a crocodile. The creature rears and knocks the cannon-sized gun from the trapper's hands. I stare in horror as the crocodile's pointed fangs elongate and sharpen by the second.

Teeth that grow? Is this real?

I breathe in another whiff of green haze, and my head spins sideways, and I stumble away from the hissing creature as it lashes at the nearest trapper. The trapper rolls away, and another one takes his place. She has an even larger weapon balanced on her shoulder.

Where did that one come from? Were the larger weapons strapped to their horseless machines?

A fistful of fire crackles in my palms, but my mind teeters. Where should I aim this? At the chomping creature with teeth as long as a spear? Or this woman aiming a weapon at—

"Elbert!" Valora's voice cuts through the smoke and clears my head. And I remember, just for a moment, who my enemy is.

I fling an armful of flames at the nearest trapper, grazing the sleeve of her coat. She yelps and pats down her arm then jerks her weapon back at the charging crocodile. One grinding click, and a piercing, artificial light spills from the snout of the weapon and cuts through the smoke, snaking around Abuelita's massive jaws.

The crocodile's mouth snaps shut, and she squirms against the power of the machine. More ropes of lightning spew from the device and grapple her body to the ground. Valora clings to Abuelita's back until she stops twitching. A swell of silence fills the clearing as everyone holds their breaths.

Another click. This time coming from the opposite direction. The man is aiming his midsized cannon at the crocodile. A net shoots from the cannon, and the force of it squashes Valora against the crocodile.

"Elbert! Run!" She screams as she squirms down Abuelita's side.

I ignore her and step forward, but something yanks me sideways. Leo's hand is gripping my arm.

"What are you doing?" He says, his face stiff with terror. "Why are you *helping* them?"

"You see that wolf over there?" I whisper, forcing myself to stay calm. "That's Lupe Padilla."

He crinkles his forehead. "What? Why...?"

"She's not just a wolf, Leo. She's a person. She's that girl's mother. And the crocodile is that girl's grandmother. They're family."

He blinks, gawking at the scene before him—Mrs. Padilla yelping and yanking against the trap on her foot, Valora breaking pieces of the net under Abuelita's teeth. Bubbles of white light burst overhead.

I shake Leo by the shoulders. "Tell me how to open that trap."

He points to the wolf. "She's that girl's... mother?"

"Yes," I say. "They're just trying to survive. They'd never hurt anyone."

He shudders. "But my boy. Remilda."

"That was a different time. A different beast. Would you ruin a family over your own grief?"

His eyes droop, and I place a hand on his shoulder, waiting. And hoping.

A loud crank is followed by a popping sound, and the trap's jaws spring open. Harold has freed Mrs. Padilla. Her guttural snarls and hulking wolf body demand the trapper's attention. They pivot their weapons toward her. Meanwhile, Valora shoves the net off an old woman.

Wait—an old woman? Abuelita must have shifted back to her human form. Harold is helping Valora drag Abuelita toward me now while the trappers fight off Mrs. Padilla.

I wave them over. "Come with me!"

When Harold and Valora drag Abuelita to my side, I point them toward home. "Take Abuelita to the farm. I'll follow you there."

I don't know if I'm speaking the truth or not.

Harold forges ahead, tugging Valora by the arm, and heads to the farm.

I clench my jaw and face the fight. Mrs. Padilla is circling the trappers, their weapons shoot sparks of light, just missing her face. The fire—*my* fire—has spread further now, up the riverbank. The flames lick the backs of the trappers as Mrs. Padilla forces them into a burning corner.

I need to stop this fire. I need to stop these trappers.

But there are only three adults. Where's the girl?

A hard knock sends me reeling to the ground. My head explodes with pain as I grit my teeth and jump to my knees.

The girl stands in front of me, a large club in her hand. "Where's the stag, Bird Boy?"

I clench my jaw. As soon as a tuft of fire gathers in my fists, I toss it in her face. She jerks back and screeches, swatting the spark to the side as if it were a wasp. The orange glow lands on a patch of dry grass.

I can't use this power right now. Not when we're surrounded by tinder.

She lunges forward and swings her club, her body following the momentum of her weapon. I jerk back, but she pivots and swings again, landing on my leg. An explosion of white light bursts from the weapon and climbs onto me.

More pain, worse than before, crackles over my body. I'm back on the dirt, rolling around as white-hot energy seizes my muscles. My body twitches and a pounding force crackles through me. I force my eyes open and stare at the girl. I expect anger to reflect in her eyes, hatred, or something evil, but all I find is a deep hunger and—a terror.

"Where is the stag?" Her voice shivers as she clicks something on the handle of her weapon, and the ropes of lightning fade away. "Tell me."

"What's your name?" I say. If this girl is going to kill me, I would like to know her name.

199

Her grip falters. "What?"

"Why are you doing this?" It feels like a fair question to ask before I die.

She blinks, and that sharp hunger I saw before seeps back into her eyes. I notice the frayed edges of her coat, the rusted metal bands on her arms, the holes in her gloves, the way her collarbone sticks out, like she hasn't eaten for days.

She swings her club again, but before lightning can shoot out the end, her head jerks forward, and she crumples into a whimper. Leo stands behind her, a metal leg brace resting in his hands. Did he just hit that girl in the back of the head?

"I told you. I don't have a mark on this one," he says to the girl.

I half-expect him to lend a hand, help me to my feet. Instead, he stares at me, that sad look on his face. "Go on home."

"I can't leave. I'm the one who started this fire. I have to stop it."

He clenches his jaw. "I saw what your Pops did at the river fire. It'll take both of you."

He saw Pops use magic at the river fire? And he never said anything?

"Why didn't you tell me?" I say.

"Go on. We don't have time to chat."

"C'mon, Leo. Come with me."

My pleas are useless. He's already turning back to the fight. And now I have to make a choice. Stay to help Mrs. Padilla fight the trappers or leave and get help to stop this fire.

And I have to choose now.

I lean into the wind, bouncing across fields of golden weeds. Fire rustles against my ears as the flames on my shoulders push me toward home. With each step, my stomach twists and a sourness seeps into my mouth. This must be doubt creeping in. I have to fix this, but deep down, I know that even with magic, it might not be enough.

Halfway through the beet fields, I catch up to the others. When we reach the barn, the sky has lightened into a pale blue. All I see is Chewbie munching on a stray pile of mown grass, trespassing again. The grounds are oddly quiet. The horses are also missing from their stables, and no one is in the fields.

Very unusual.

When we crack open the back door, more silence greets us. We walk past a cold wood-burning stove in the kitchen, and we help Abuelita wobble into a chair.

"Is she going to be okay?" I examine Abuelita's listless face. Angry welts wrap around her arms and legs. "We have an herb garden if you need it," I say to Valora.

"I know."

That's right. She's stolen from that garden.

"I'm going to make a salve," she says. "Then I'm going back."

She's going back? Into the fire? "No, Valora, that's a bad—"

She points a scowl at me, and my words die in my mouth. "Today is not the day I let you save me, Pollo."

"Okay." I shift past them.

"Where are you going?" Harold calls. "We need your help."

"We need Pops," I say as I head for the hallway.

Chapter Thirty-Three

"Elbert, is that you out there?" Pops's voice muffles through the door before I push it open.

I tighten my jaw and step quickly into the musty room. Pops is sitting upright with grandpa's journal cracked open in his lap. I open my mouth, ready to ask for help, but then I see his tired, sad face.

"You okay, Pops?" I say, standing just out of arm's reach. He's clearly in pain, most likely grieving Juniper's memory. I can pause, let him gather himself, but only for a moment.

Pops presses a hand against his cheek and grunts, and a tear slides down his finger. "I was just reading."

I sneak a glance and recognize the handwriting of the journal entry. "You wrote that?"

He nods. "I miss her so much. Sometimes it's the strongest emotion I have, the pain I feel when I think of her."

A sadness swells in me, but I push it aside. I don't have time to dwell on the pain of Juniper. *We* don't have time for it.

"Pops, can you get up? We need—"

"Don't run from the things that hurt you, Elby," he cuts

me off. "I've been doing it, too. For too long. It's time for you to slow down."

He leans forward and grips my shoulders, and a powerful force weighs me down—stronger than a human hand. This could only be magic.

"What are you doing?" I strain to speak. "What is this?"

"It's time for you to decide, Son. Will you take your magic, or ignore it until the flame snuffs out? What is holding you back?"

I forget about Abuelita's battered form and Mrs. Padilla's snarling wolf. I forget about the fire. All I can think about is the pain—the burden—of what comes with this magic.

"What is holding you back, Elby?" Pops says again.

My pattering heartbeat slows, and then I think of her. Juniper.

I've been avoiding this magic, yes, but I've been avoiding her, too. Until recently, I'd kept everything locked inside a corner of my mind. But for the past few weeks, maybe even months, a sickness has lingered with me, and a weak sadness, a numb helplessness, a sour anger.

This is what a curse feels like.

Shame stings my side as guilt climbs back into my thoughts. My power comes from the same substance that ended my sister's life—fire. Every time I pull a spark into my fists, deep down, I remember this guilt. And that's why it's always felt so wrong. Why it's always felt like a curse.

I've been carrying a curse, and now I finally understand. It was never the fire, the feathers, not even the pain of watching Pops grieve. I've been ignoring it for so long, I never noticed until now.

It was always her.

A light knock taps against the door, but I don't have the sense to respond.

"Yes?" Pops says, his voice tight with surprise. "Someone

else is here?" he whispers to me.

Valora cracks the door open and peeks her head inside.

Pops gasps. "You're, *you're…*"

She slides her gaze to me. "Is he okay?"

"Yes. I'm perfectly fine," Pops answers. "But you're a shapeshifter, aren't you?"

She ignores his questions and points at me. "No, is Elbert okay?"

No. I'm not okay. The magic in Pops's hands weighs like a pile of rocks, and this curse is squeezing my throat. Old, ugly thoughts are climbing back and scattering my last bit of hope. This magic will ruin me. It will ruin everyone.

Cool, soft hands press against my temples, easing the burden of Pop's magic. Dark eyes—Valora's eyes—spark green as she peers into my face. "What's wrong?"

I drag in a breath. "I can't… breathe," I swallow down the sob bobbing in my throat.

Valora glances back at Pops, as if calculating how much she can trust him, then her piercing eyes dart back to me. "Remember this, Elbert. Your magic is *good*."

I shake my head. "It's bad, Valora. It's always been bad."

Pops sniffles. He knows. I waited years to grow strong enough to protect the ones I love, but now I'm dangerous. This fire burns. It's too much.

"I don't want this magic, Pops," I say. "It's too dangerous."

"Is that your final choice?" He sounds disappointed.

Valora leans in, her nose brushing mine. "Listen to me, Pollo. Yes, you're dangerous. We're all dangerous. But remember the good things you can do."

Good things? What good things?

She huffs, and I sense her irritation creeping in. "You don't just make fire, Elbert. You also take it away."

Slowly, her words sink in. She's right. The river fire on the fourth of July, I was pulling flames *toward* me. I don't just make fire. I *control* it. I can make it go away.

Maybe that's why my spark kept growing. Somewhere deep, deeper than my doubt and self-disgust, I was hoping this magic would do something good. Like protect a younger brother.

This fear of burning things like a bedsheet, a best friend's shirt, the people I love—it starts to crack. And for the first time, I see the whole truth. My magic can be good. It can protect. Why didn't I see this before?

I brush away the tears crawling down my face and wipe my hands on the front of my shirt. I pause, realizing my cheeks are cool and fresh, not stinging with pain. I'm reminded of what Leo said, about the time grief had taken over his life. Something about sadness. When you're sad, you believe things that aren't true. This magic was only a curse because I believed it was.

"She's right, Elbert," Pops says. "I forgot for a while—the nature of our magic. This fire in us protects. But sometimes we fail."

Valora nods. "Yes, sometimes. Because we're human."

Human.

All this time, I simply wanted to be back to normal—back to human. But my human side also weakens me. Makes me vulnerable.

"But Mamá always says to hold on to my human side," Valora says. "Never let the wild side grow too far, or you won't find your way back home."

"She's right," Pops says. "This magic in you—it's important. It can do good things."

The words are simple, but deep down, I feel myself believing them. This magic can do good, but I'm human. Sometimes I won't be strong enough. But that's just how it is. That's what it means to be—normal.

A wave of relief washes over me. For the first time since Juniper's death, the hate and bitterness toward my younger, helpless self falls away. The resentment toward my unpredictable magic fades.

I turn back to Pops. "Okay," I say. "I'm ready for this magic."

Valora's eyes widen. "Are you going to spark, Elbert?"

Pops squeezes my shoulders, and I rest my hands on his. As soon as our fingers touch, something pops between them. A spark. My skin starts to burn, almost itch. What once felt like a burden now feels like a pool of energy pouring into me. It grows stronger, wilder. A wind circles us and stokes the flames bursting from my skin. I light up like a torch, burning right here in the bedroom. Valora is shouting. Probably wants me to stop. But I can't stop the magic tearing through my limbs and firing through my nerves. I'm growing. I'm changing.

This is good. This is my blessing.

The rustling energy moves through my muscles and bones —and grows. And even though I'm still afraid, I welcome this magic into my soul.

Finally, the storm wanes, and I find myself on the ground. I don't remember how I got here. I must have fallen at some point.

Valora's scowling face hovers over me. "You look different."

She pulls me to my feet and tugs me away from the body-sized burn mark on the floor.

"What was that?" I say.

Why are they staring at me like I'm still on fire?

Harold bumps through the door with a bowl full of dark sludge—for Abuelita's wounds, most likely. He blinks at me and gasps. "Elbert, you're a *boy*."

It takes a minute for Harold's words to sink in. I hold up

one of my arms and trace a finger over featherless, spongy skin. I rub my face. Smooth, except for the sticky, half-dried trails of tears. I glance down at my stubby toes, each paired with translucent shells—toenails! It feels and looks so strange—like my body made a mistake.

Mistake. Did I just lose everything? My magic? My abilities? The thought hurts more than I expect.

"Is it gone?" I whisper, searching my body. What am I looking for? An on-switch?

Valora laughs. "No! Elbert, of course not. The magic is still there. Inside you."

I swallow, focusing on my heartbeat, and then I feel it—a fire nestled inside me.

Pops pounds his hands together. "Son! You finished the spell. You've finally accepted your magic."

Valora huffs. "Okay, okay. Yes, he has. But we have to go now." She yanks my arm, but I stay put. "Hurry up, Elbert. Mamá is out there."

All at once, everything from before rushes back to me—Abuelita, Mrs. Padilla still fighting the trappers, and the fire.

"Yes, Pops. We need to go."

"Why?" Pops says as he creaks to his feet.

"We'll explain as we go," Valora says and waves a hand to keep moving.

"Okay, but I won't be moving fast like I used to," he says and hobbles to the door.

Fast? When has Pops ever moved fast?

Pops thumps through the hallway, and I hear Abuelita cough and murmur in the other room.

"Who's that?" Pops whispers back to Harold.

"Another friend," Harold says. "She's a crocodile."

I'm the last to join everyone in the living room, and I notice Abuelita is on her feet, teetering but upright. My heart leaps into my throat. She's awake! She's okay.

Her eyes meet mine. "Elberto," She says something in Spanish and grins, pointing at me.

"You finished your spell," Valora translates. "You're not just part human and part phoenix. You are all human, all phoenix."

Abuelita reaches for me, and as I walk over, a waft of smoke tickles my nose. I glance out the window. On the horizon, a gray haze blends into the clouds. The fire has grown large enough to scatter the birds.

"Okay, now we really have to go," I say, fear digging into my side. We already took so much time. "We have to go *now*."

"Is that a wildfire I'm smelling?" Pops says.

My stomach flops as I realize we have no river to stop this fire. That old, shrinking fear threatens to take over, but this time, I stomp it down.

We must stop it. Even if I have to use magic.

"Yes, that's why we keep saying 'let's go, let's go,'" Valora says.

"I started a fire. By the river." I bend my head, avoiding the faces around me. "That's why we came here for you, Pops. We need your help."

Pops stops and gasps. "You found Finn, right?" He twists his neck to the window. "Where is everyone? They're back, right?"

"What?" My heart starts pattering. "Is Finn out there? Why didn't you tell me?"

Pops crinkles his forehead. "I thought you knew he left. You weren't here this morning, neither was Finn. We thought you went after him. You didn't come back, so Mom and the others went out looking. I thought since you were back, you'd found him, but if you don't know he's gone off—That means everyone's still out there."

Chapter Thirty-Four

Valora rushes out the door while Pops and I straggle behind. His raspy breaths land hard on my ears, adding to the lump of panic in my stomach. Harold leaps past us, Abuelita clinging to his back.

"What are you doing, Harold?" Valora growls. "Take Abuelita home. She needs to rest."

"No." Abuelita grunts and points. "You... need *me*."

Valora's eyes flash emerald fire. "Take her home, Harold. Or I'll put a hex on you."

Harold shrugs, still hopping along. "I do what she wants. She can turn into a crocodile and bite me to bits. You're just a girl."

Harold might as well have thrown dirt in Valora's face. She scoffs at him, then dives toward the smoke, her feet bouncing across the earth, like stones skimming water—faster than any human speed. I want to keep pace with her, but I'd have to rustle up handfuls of fire and draw strength from the flames. I don't want to burn Pops.

Oh, that's right. Pops doesn't burn.

Flames circle my arms and flicker past my shoulders, and

Pops and I press into the chafing wind—the same wind that is coaxing the fire up the muddy riverbed. I pump my legs harder as fresh bodies of smoke curl to the sky.

How will Pops and I stop this? The riverbed is dry. Where are we going to send this fire?

We reach the riverbed, but no one is here. No Leo, no trappers for hire, no magic wolf. Just a crackling carpet of flames climbing up the countryside. Valora throws herself down the incline and scrambles up the rise, heading for the hills.

"Wait!" I cry. "I need your help."

"Andrés and Mamá first!" Valora shouts, but she staggers to a stop.

I lean Pops against a boulder and pull Valora to the side. "We need your help to stop this fire."

"No, Elbert, I need to find my family. You can stop this fire." She turns on her heels.

I tug her arm and spin her back. "I can't do it without you." My mind reels, grasping for ideas. "You know the flames are too dangerous for you. Let me find them. Then you can help Pops fight the fire."

She blinks angrily, then glances at the glowing fields. I can already see the flush in her cheeks. Fire is her weakness. I have to do this. She knows it.

"This is the time, Valora." I grip her shoulders.

"Time for what, Pollo?" She says, her muscles turning to stone under my grip. Her magic is already making her stronger.

"It's time to let me save you." I grin.

"Hurry then," she says, a smile tugging at her mouth. Then she huffs. "Ay, Elbert, no." She wags a finger. "I'm saving *you*."

Harold stumbles in between us and lowers Abuelita to the dirt. To show her thanks, the old woman pats Harold on the back as he gasps for air. Then she totters to the bank of the dusty river.

"Ay, Harold!" Valora hisses. "Why don't you listen? She shouldn't be here."

Harold pants for breath and wheezes out a handful of words. "Miss Crocodile... says... there's something..."

Valora rolls her eyes.

A cracking sound, like rocks tumbling off a cliff, snags our attention. There is Abuelita, her arms glowing with green fire. A pile of mud the size of a cow hovers above her fingertips. She jerks her arms, and the mud squelches onto a patch of burning grass. When I look back to the riverbed, I see a puddle of water where the mud used to be. She's carving a trench, deep enough to reach water.

Abuelita waves at Valora. "M'ija." She pauses and nods. "You need *me*."

I don't have time to gather something to say. I don't have time to see if Pops can rise to his legs or drag flames to the riverbed. I've already waited too long. It's time for me to find the others.

Who is still out there?

I clamor up the rise and dive into the blackened haze, following the trails of smoke. Cords of light dance before my eyes. They eat paths along the dried grasses and up the brittle backs of trees.

"Finn! Where are you? *Finn*!"

I hear nothing, just the thudding of my heart and the spitting flames. I throw myself into the crackling earth and keep shouting names.

"Andrés! Mrs. Padilla! Finn!" I even call Leo's name. I

know he's got a new leg, but he can't be *that* fast. Did he chase the wolf or run from the fire?

"Peto! Vida!" They probably saw the smoke and ran back to the farm, but the pit in my stomach isn't so sure.

Only the sound of burning grasses calls back.

"Finn! Answer me! *Finn!*" After clawing and diving through the smoky wasteland, I lose my sense of direction. I pause, waiting for my galloping heart to slow down. Then I listen.

Nothing. Just me and the fire crunching on its meal.

Then I remember the dream. The one that came to me while the Padilla women rescued me from the river. The one where fire crawls along the earth, and I turn into fire—a phoenix. It's time to fulfill this dream.

And yes. I will fly.

A rush of energy lifts inside me, and for the first time in a very long time, I feel light. Lighter than bones. Lighter than sadness or disappointments. I gather the small bit of hope that's been growing inside me and ask it to believe in something more. Something that will carry me above the noise and the blinding haze, above the tops of trees, until my feet brush the backs of breezes, and all that surrounds me is the sky.

And I open my eyes.

"Woah!" The words pop out of my mouth as I teeter in the wind.

It worked! I can't believe it. How is this happening?

I reach for a cloud, and something presses against my shoulder blades. Warm like a pair of hands. The pressure eases, then pushes down again.

What's moving on my back?

A scarlet flag waves in the corner of my eye. But that's not a flag. I crane my neck to get a better look.

Those are wings! *My* wings, climbing up the sky. Wow!

This thought would have terrified me only a handful of days ago, but now it's exciting.

I stumble through the waves of gushing winds before I get a good sense of how to steer and angle my body. I realize that most of my control comes from focusing my mind and the position of my arms. Arms forward, I go in the direction they are pointed. Arms back, I slow down.

I sweep as low to the ground as possible without knocking into a tree branch, and I call out Finn's name at every turn. Then I circle closer to the river and notice more people have joined us in taming the fire. I recognize Peto and Vida on horseback carrying a wagon full of barrels of water. Further up the river is another band of men. One of them might be Daichi.

Where is Mrs. Padilla? And the trappers?

I continue weaving along the treetops, slowly pulling further away from the river. At one point, I spot a pair of antlers shifting through the brush. Andrés. Is he searching for something? I'm not sure what, but I don't have time to figure out how to land on the ground *and* convince Andrés to shift back to human form just so he can tell me what he's doing.

I skim past the buck and head deeper into the hills. "Finn! Where are you? Can you hear me?" I call these same three phrases over and over until my voice grows hoarse, and the warm spot between my shoulder blades starts to ache.

Then I notice a small shadow standing on a golden hillside. I squint and veer toward the lone figure, now waving his arms and jumping—and shouting back.

"I'm here!" A high-pitched squeal reaches my ears.

"Finn!" I call. Another burst of fire wraps my body and pushes me forward. Almost there. Just up this rise.

But how do I land?

Hard on my butt. That's how I land.

I skid a trail through the grass, and when I slow to a stop, I slump over the ground, letting the wind smear away my fiery wings. And I'm back to average again.

"Elbert?" Finn croaks. Bits of ash stick to the tears on his face. He's probably been crying for a while now.

"I know," I say and wrap my arms around his shivering body, "I can fly."

Finn coughs in my ear. It could be a laugh. "Yes. But I was going to say you look like a boy."

"You scared me half to death. What are you doing so far away from home?"

"I walked out here in my sleep. You know that."

"When you see her in your dreams, Finn, you shouldn't follow. It's not safe." I shudder, trying not to imagine what could have happened.

His eyes widen, and he cocks his head to the side. "I don't follow her," he says. "She follows *me*. And then she leads me to safety. But today she took me a different way." He taps his finger on his chin, trying to make sense of something.

Is this true? Finn wanders out into the dark, and then Juniper finds him—and brings him *home*? Should I be thanking this imaginary friend for saving my little brother's life? But today is different. Finn says she didn't take him home today. Why not? If I believed in imaginary friends, I'd say Juniper led Finn away from the fire.

"It's okay," he says, his voice deep, like he's holding back tears. "I won't be seeing her anymore."

"Really?" I say, hopeful. "Are you letting her go?"

"No," he says. "She's letting *me* go. This was the last time we got to play."

The eerie words bring a mix of unease and relief, and for a moment, my doubts about Juniper's ghost soften.

I pat his shoulder as he hunches over his knees. "I'm sorry, Buddy."

He rubs his eyes. "Me, too."

"I don't believe in ghosts or imaginary friends, but I'll say this." I grin. "If you didn't come out here this far, you might've got lost in the fire. But you're safe now. Thank heavens."

"Thank Juniper."

That's not what I meant, but I won't fight it. Instead, I hold out a hand and pull him to his feet. "We need to go."

When I assess the burning grasses, I spot a hulking shadow sauntering between the clouds of smoke.

What is that?

"Is that Mr. Deer?" Finn gasps.

The shadow moves closer, and the familiar arch of antlers slips through the gloom.

"Yes, his name is Andrés," I say.

"I know that. He's my friend."

Chapter Thirty-Five

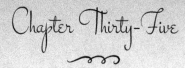

Finn climbs on the stag's back as if he's done this many times.

"I've done this many times," he announces.

After I shut my gaping mouth, I climb beside him.

"You can grab his antlers. He's okay with that," Finn says.

I pause and shake my head in disbelief. "How do you know all this?"

"He's caught me sleepwalking a few times. On the nights you're not around." Finn smirks like he's proud to have his own secret. "Juni usually leads me to him."

I'm short on words, so I reach for the smooth surface of Andrés's antlers. The stag twitches his ears and lurches down the hill, veering past rocks and shrubs. I dip forward with each rise, much like riding a horse bareback. I'm glad I've got something to hold onto, even if they are shaped like branches.

Once we reach level ground, Andrés charges forward. Finn squeezes my stomach as we dive into a wall of smoke.

I can't see anything. Not at first. But I can hear the hiss of fire as it devours the land and belches out smoke. The bitter smell of ash and dirt clogs my nose.

"You okay, Finn?" I call over my shoulder.

He squeezes my waist and coughs.

I'll take that as a "yes."

We bump along, swerving through billows of smoke. As the path darkens, Andrés charges forward without hesitation. Maybe it's because he's roamed these hills many times, day and night. Maybe he knows where every shrub, rock, and tree belong.

"Help!" A voice cuts across the clearing.

"Did you hear that?" Finn asks, then coughs. "Sounds like an old man."

"Help!"

Andrés slows, and the muscles in his shoulders tighten.

"It's coming from there," I say and point past the stag's nose.

Wait. What have I just done? That's probably Leo's voice. And I've just pointed Andrés to the man who's trying to capture him. But at the same time, I don't want Leo to *die*. The smoke alone could suffocate him if the flames don't eat him alive.

Maybe I can still talk some sense into the old man. I hope he isn't carrying any of those fancy weapons.

"Where are you?" Finn calls out.

Andrés steps past a shrub glimmering orange with fire, and we see Leo stumbling down a slope. A woman hangs over his shoulders, unconscious.

"Mrs. Padilla! Are you okay?" I glare at Leo. "What did you do?"

"Leo! That you?" Finn shrieks.

Leo doesn't run like I expect him to. He stands there with Mrs. Padilla in his arms, a grimace darkening his face. Is he afraid? What did he do?

"Elbert!" he calls. "The wolf changed into this person. And she's got these dark welts. She's barely breathing."

His confusion would make sense, except he's the one who

put the mark on the Padilla family. Doesn't he know how shapeshifters work?

"Haven't you done this before?" I say, leaping to the ground. "You're a trapper."

I pull Mrs. Padilla off Leo's shoulders. Her hands tighten around my arm, then fall limp.

"I never hunted," Leo rasps in my ear. "My leg always held me back. I always thought they were humans too far gone into the wild. You know, feral."

I blink, shocked that he would think this about the Padilla family. Then I notice a trail of black welts climbing up Mrs. Padilla's arms. Her breathing comes in short gasps. "What did you do, Leo?" I glare at him until the truth sinks in.

Not Leo. It was me. I started this fire. This is the reason I told Valora not to come. But Mrs. Padilla can't stand the heat either.

But why hasn't Andrés flinched every time he runs past the burning brush? I turn back to Andrés, and for the first time, I notice the burn marks tracing his legs and grazing his belly. It's a wonder he's still standing.

He'll need to stand for a little longer.

I swing Mrs. Padilla onto Andrés's back. "Hold fast," I tell Finn. "Don't let her slide."

Finn nods and grips her waist, a stern look in his eyes. In this moment, he looks older than before.

I suck in a breath and hold out a hand to Leo. "You, too, old man. Let's go."

I hope I'm not making a mistake.

"No, Son, I can't fit on there. Women and children first." The old man crosses his arms, and a glowing tree limb lands hard on his right. Fire hisses at his feet. Still, he won't budge.

I snatch a clammy, shaking hand. "Come on, Leo. We have to go."

The lights in his eyes fade, like he's slipped into a sad memory.

"You can't just stay here." I tug his arm again.

"Go on, boy. I'm done here."

Done here? What does that mean? I don't have time for this. Neither does Andrés. Even as Leo leaps over a burning shrub and starts running away, Andrés bounds across the charred grasses and angles for him. I race behind, watching as the stag dips his wreath of antlers and scoops up Leo mid-stride. Leo bellows and shrieks as he clings to Andrés while the stag charges into a wall of smoke.

I gather a cord of flames from the brush and clench it in my fists. The heat gives me the strength to follow Andrés. The stag pulls ahead, weaving his way down the countryside, but I can hear him wheezing, sharp and raspy, like he's got something stuck in his throat.

We run this way, for what feels like hours, Andrés wheezing ahead with Finn and Mrs. Padilla on his back and Leo clinging to his antlers. How much longer can he go?

I hope we're almost there.

Then the sound of gunfire echoes through the trees, and I stutter to a stop.

"Andrés!" I scream. "FINN!"

I jump back into a sprint, and before I know it, a cloud of green smoke tumbles over me.

Chapter Thirty-Six

The green smoke burrows into my face and tickles my ears, but the sting is not as harsh, and my thoughts are not as scattered. Not like before. I can deal with this. I must be building a tolerance to the smoke. It's about time. I've been sprayed several times in one day. But right now my mind, my body—everything still works.

Oh. Except for my legs. They're crumpling to the ground.

I grit my teeth and stumble into a small clearing ringed with a red-haired family. They've shrugged off their coats, and now they clutch their electric-powered weapons. They edge closer to a boy, limp on the ground.

"Get away!" I scream. "Leave them alone!"

Finn. Andrés. Leo. Mrs. Padilla is there, too. All of them are in danger now.

The man balances his mid-sized cannon and speaks behind his mask. "Mark or no mark. We're taking in our catches."

Leo cocks his gun and aims at the woman with red hair. "You take one of ours, we'll take one of yours."

One of ours. Did Leo just take our side?

"I *will* shoot," he says and scrapes to his feet. "And this one over here is made of fire." He nods to me. "He'll finish you off."

The red-haired trapper bristles, but he doesn't move.

Leo aims his weapon at the woman. "Are you sure it's worth the trade? Life for a life?"

A breeze hurries past, and the trappers consider Leo's threat. Then, without the slightest trembling, the man lowers his weapon, as do the woman and the girl. Leo lets his gun drift back to the ground as well.

A dark shadow weaves to my right, just up the rise. It's a new beast, one I've never seen before, with a pair of antlers the size of trees. A stag. A female—with antlers.

"What happened?" The girl with the red hair glances back at Andrés. "Did the stag escape us?" She points to the deer in the distance. "It's over there now, Papa."

The man and woman glance at one another and nod. Before I can shout a warning, the trappers jump into a sprint, heading for the new target.

"Valora!" Andrés cries, tears streaming down his face. He staggers to his feet, but his legs are black, just like Mrs. Padilla. He won't be running anytime soon. That's not good. We still need to get them out of here. I throw Mrs. Padilla's arm over my neck and hold out a hand to Andrés, but he doesn't take it.

"We'll find her. She's faster than them, Andrés. She knows what to do."

I hope it's true, but Valora has never shifted before. Will she hold onto her human mind or get lost in the wild thoughts of a stag? All my nerves want to chase her down and protect her.

But I can't. I have to stop this awful fire.

"Help him, please," I say to Finn, passing his small hand to Andrés. This time, Andrés accepts.

I don't have to walk far before Peto and a couple of other men break into the clearing. They've got rags pressed to their mouths. Finn lets go of Andrés and latches onto his brother while a couple of men take over carrying Mrs. Padilla and Andrés. I think they're saying something about the river—that it's only a few more steps away. Peto gives me a stern nod. No need to exchange words. It's obvious chattering is not the priority.

"You ready, old man?" I say to Leo, holding out a hand.

"You don't have time for this, Elbert. You need to stop this fire." At first, I think he's joking, but his face is hard as flint.

Is he joking?

"Let me help you to the river, first," I insist.

He bends and tugs his pantleg above his knee and unlatches several springs. With a small whir, the leg brace pops clean off.

"Stop wasting time with me," he says, holding out the brace.

"What are you doing?" I get that he's turning away from his trapper lifestyle, but this is a bit extravagant.

"Give this to your pops. He'll need it if he's going to help you stop this blaze."

"How did you see Pops use his magic? I thought no one was around."

He taps the goggles fastened to his head. "I saw him at the picnic."

"And you didn't say anything?"

"Stop wasting time, Elbert. Go give this to your Pops." He shoves me toward the river.

Leo's right. This fire has only grown worse, and I'll need Pops on his feet if we're going to have a chance. But I'm not going to just leave Leo here with his lame leg. I sling his arm over my shoulder and drag him through the worst of the flames, closer to the river's edge.

"I'm sorry, son. I didn't know." His voice rattles in my ear. "I never realized they were real people. I'm sorry. Sorry."

I squeeze his bony shoulder and prepare to head off alone. He'll be safe enough where he is. "It's okay, Leo," I say. "You did the right thing. In the end."

His watery blue eyes lock onto mine. "You know, he'd be a bit older than you... if he were still alive."

I try not to think about the dark tone in the old man's voice. Instead, I race along the riverbed, straight for Pops. When I glance back, Leo is gone.

I get further upriver and see that the ditch has grown. But even with Abuelita's powers, the water is not that deep, not quite wide enough. The fire is still too big. It's crawling over stretches of blond prairie grass and reaching for the fields now, toward the crops and homes.

I squint downriver and pick out bodies moving back and forth. Some are carrying buckets, and some are loading horses with pots of water. There's Andrés, still in human form, and Mrs. Padilla is resting against the riverbank, her hands stirring to her forehead. I hope that means she's okay. I wonder if she saw what her daughter did to save our lives.

I tighten my grip on Leo's brace and dash toward Pops. Another monstrous pile of smoke oozes down the hillside. The ground is uneven under my average feet, and for the first time, I miss having leathery, misshapen toes.

Pops clenches his arms and yanks a patch of fire down to the river. When his gaze lands on me, he waves me over. "Did you find Finn?"

"Yes," I say, noting the creases in his forehead and a layer of soot smeared across his face. "Are you getting tired?"

"The fire's too big," he says, ignoring my question. "We've contained some, but it's growing. And I can only do so much."

"Well, I'm here now. I can help."

I hold up Leo's brace. "This is for you. From Leo."

"What is it?" Pops frowns.

I lift the hem of Pop's pants and latch on Leo's leg brace. The nobs click tight around his calf, and a whirring sound starts drumming softly. I hope that means it's working.

"What did you—"

"—Can you walk?"

He juts his leg forward, and the brace creaks, holding him upright. "I can walk." His mustache bends into a smile, and he peers at the gritty sky. "C'mon, Elby. Let's fight this beast."

Then, before I can sense what he's about to do, he marches toward the smoke. He reaches a fringe of crackling trees, stretches out his arms, and greets the flames like an old friend.

I throw myself into the flickering orange forest and wrap tongues of fire around my arms. Soon, my load of fire grows large, almost beyond my grip, so I head back to the river and hope for a miracle.

But the winds have other plans.

I cross through a small clearing, and I'm caught wrestling with a strong gust. The sharp breeze snatches a tendril of fire from my arms and throws it to the ground. The orange glow sinks into the brush, then climbs up a tree.

I have to get out of here.

I slip into the cover of trees, careful to avoid the low-hanging branches. A throbbing pain pulses at the base of my head, but no more stray tendrils have lost their way. I slide past a shaggy willow and leap over a hedge until I'm back to the river. Before the wind whips into another frenzy, I throw my load of fire into the oozing water. Vapors rise on impact as the water quenches the flames.

Abuelita continues digging trenches in the mud. She flings another armful of dirt against a burning treetop. I notice Peto and Daichi and a few more men carrying buckets of water from the river.

It's inspiring, watching them battling this fire, braving the heat and ash, but it's pointless. The flames have stretched too far. At this rate, the smoke will choke them all to death. They're going to die trying to stop *my* fire. The thought alone makes me want to sink into the earth.

A hand grips my shoulder. It's Pops, his face tight with a smile. Something's hiding in his eyes. "I'm proud of you, Son."

Why do his words sound like a goodbye?

"I'm going to leave," he says, "and I don't want you to follow."

"Where are you going?" A spark of worry bites my chest.

He pauses and leans as if to consider answering my question. Instead, he squeezes my shoulder and says something else. "I'm sorry it took me so long to realize..." His voice falters, and I hold my tongue, hoping he'll go on and explain himself. But he just stares at me.

This is Pops—feeling his way through a moment, letting the silence do all the talking. And slowly, as he scrounges for words, I notice how much he has changed. He looks lighter, fuller. He looks like me.

"I'm sorry it took so long to realize how I should use this... gift," he says.

His words are full of heart, but that does not excuse his threat to leave. Please don't say something about sacrifice and dying for the ones you love.

He dips his head down and clenches his jaw.

"What is it?" I demand.

"It's time for me to use this gift to protect you. Like I should have been doing all along."

Tears swim in his glowing, fiery eyes. And with one swift motion, he turns his back to me and opens his broad arms. A hissing wind gathers and hoists him into the air. A burst of golden light pours from his palms, his eyes, and the tips of his toes. The light is so striking, I have to shield my eyes. When the light fades, Pops is still hanging above the ground, but now his body has transformed into a massive creature of scarlet-orange feathers, leathery and pointed talons for his feet, and wings of fire.

"Fénix!" Abuelita's voice echoes from across the ditch. Joy brightens her face.

Fear twists my insides.

"No! Pops, *no!*" He's shifting into a phoenix, slipping away from his humanity and embracing the wild. This is dangerous. Our magic isn't like earth magic. Fire magic eats us up when we get too close. It consumes our sense of what we know and love.

If he turns into the phoenix, he might not find his way back home.

His giant, bird-like body climbs up the pillars of smoke, and I gather what fire I have left in my chest and stoke the flickering spark into a flame. I stretch my arms until the fire grows into wings. I push into the air and follow Pops into the mountain of smoke.

Flying through smoke reminds me of diving to the bottom of a lake, except here I'm surrounded by a gray haze. Down below, pinkish-orange light bubbles underneath a gray blanket.

I catch sight of Pops dipping low until his phoenix body grazes the treetops. He pulls orange ribbons of fire from underneath the mass of smoke. It climbs onto his back, latches to his whiplike tail, and forms a ring, much like when he gathered fire around his arm the night of the church picnic. He dives back and forth, pulling fire off the treetops and grasses. The fire at the base of his tail continues to grow as he glides up and down the countryside and snatches flames from the ground with a powerful force of magic. Finally, all that's left are lingering clouds of ash.

I wait for him to head back so he can dive into the canal and throw his fiery load into the river. But I know he won't. He's too big for that canal. The wind would steal the flames off his tail and throw them into the trees. And we'd be back where we started, scrambling to collect the fire.

Instead, he veers due west. Toward the ocean.

I lift above the haze and follow. We soar high enough to brush the bellies of clouds, and with the harsh winds, the fire grows, strong as ever.

We need something more. We need water. A lot of water.

A few minutes pass, and we clear the smoke. In the distance, I spot the coast. I've never seen the ocean this way, how it slides onto the shore, then slips backward.

Pops teeters and dips. He must be tiring.

When he slips down a second time, I angle forward, descending low enough to fly underneath his belly. He dips down again, but this time, I lift my hands and push him up. Gradually, Pops leans his full weight on me. At this angle, it's difficult to fly as fast, or as far, but we're almost there. Fields of sand pass under my feet.

Almost there.

We're dipping low, and my toes skim the ground.

Not yet.

Finally, we reach mud. We reach foam. And the giant fiery phoenix dives into the ocean's curling jaws. His golden wings sizzle and disappear into vapor as he's swallowed by the sea.

Chapter Thirty-Seven

It's mid-September and a special day for all of us, so I bring Chewbie a handful of wildflowers, the purple ones sprinkled with white buds. I'm not sure if they will spoil her appetite, or worse, poison her, so I tuck them inside the cowbell strap, away from her chomping lips.

"You look nice," I murmur, warming my hand on her forehead where she's been facing the sun.

It's been weeks now since Pops hurled himself into the sea. I still remember the salty spray, the fire glowing around his tail, and the way he twisted under the arms of the waves. And all the flames, the feathers—the phoenix—disappeared into a cloud of smoke. Leaving behind a water-burned man, his mind lost to the wild.

I wonder when he lost himself to the phoenix. There must have been a part of him that held on and pushed himself into those waters. Why else would a phoenix fly into the ocean?

Chewbie nudges my hand, reminding me of her presence. I scratch the backs of her ears. "He doesn't remember us yet. Doesn't remember much of anything," I say, feeling the weight of Pops's sacrifice. He traded everything to save us. Because of the fire that should have never left my hands.

Getting home that day was nothing short of a miracle. After Pops dove into the water, he changed back to his human form, but he was unconscious—or lost to the wild—I'm not sure which. I sloshed into the waves and dragged his limp body from the currents. The ocean mist felt like needles against my skin, the rolling tide like rocks pelting my legs. The next thing I knew, I was on my back, my body convulsing. Pops slumped beside me.

We twitched in the mud for what felt like hours, waiting for someone to drag us to dry land. Neither one of us had the strength to move as the tide slowly ebbed away from the shore, and our bodies sucked deeper into the clay.

Fuzzy Lips found us first. I believe that horse has some magical intuition. He could find Pops in a windstorm in the center of a volcano.

Peto says he saw Pops and me glowing in the sky, and he followed us toward the ocean. He and Fuzzy Lips ambled up the shoreline until they found us squirming in the mud. I don't remember this part, but Peto hoisted me onto Fuzzy Lips's saddle and draped Pops over his back. Then more help arrived.

Daichi came with a cart padded with blankets and pillows. I remember this part. I even asked Daichi what his blankets were made of. They felt soft, like butter.

"Silk," he said.

That's the last thing he said to me before he headed north to elope with Vida. They should arrive home by train today, so we can celebrate their marriage. I didn't know this, but it's illegal for a Japanese man to marry a European woman here in California. But not in the state of Washington.

Peto already left to meet them at the station while Jorm and Trinna have been helping Mom cook up a feast. We delivered invitations to half the town, including a letter that I dropped off at Leo's shop. Not that we expect him to show up. No one has seen him since the fire. Some say he got swallowed up by the flames, others claim they saw him board a train headed east. I hope he's on his way to Missouri, where his family disappeared.

A pinch at my elbow makes my heart jump. "Mom! Don't scare me like that." I rub my elbow even though it doesn't hurt. Normally, I'd hear the crunch of her footsteps before I saw her. I must have been deep in thought.

She pinches me again and bops me on the head. "Don't talk to your mama that way. There's someone here to see you."

"Who is it?" My heart stretches against my ribs as I hope for the impossible. Please, let it be *her*. Let it be Valora. But I know better. Valora is gone. And so are Abuelita, Mrs. Padilla, and Andrés. I'm not sure when or how, but they disappeared without leaving a word or a note. All I have is Valora's flower, still warm, still fresh. I hope that means she's safe. I've got nothing else to tell me otherwise. I can't pretend it doesn't hurt.

"It's Mr. Halifax," Mom says.

I bury my face under a hand and roll my eyes. "No, thank you."

"You'll want to hear what he has to say."

I groan at the man waddling up the path, bowler hat in one arm, a book in the other.

"Hello, Elbert." He speaks carefully, like I'm a feather ready to blow away.

I *wish* I were a feather that could blow away.

He clears his throat, and for a moment he's speechless. I welcome the silence. Maybe he'll leave me alone.

Then he speaks. "I want to show you something. But we'll have to go... see *him*."

I shudder. I don't want to see Pops. Not the way he is. Not when I remember who he once was.

"I can't," I say.

Mr. Halifax sighs. "I know, but remember. Your mum hired me to search for a cure."

"You can't cure him. He's dead."

His face pinches in surprise when I say the word "dead." I wish we'd all say it. Acknowledge the truth. Pops is never coming back.

Mr. Halifax holds up a book called *Mythos of the Phoenix* and opens to the beginning of a chapter. "I found a new book," He says with a sparkle in his eye. "Chapter Twelve: How to Raise a Phoenix."

We find Pops in the barn, sitting on a crate. He's holding a handful of hay out to Fuzzy Lips. The horse snorts and shakes his head. My guess is Pops has been feeding him bites all morning, and Fuzzy's had his fill, but he's too polite to say anything.

"Thank you, Mr. Halifax," I say, pausing just outside the entrance. "But do you mind?"

"Of course, Elbert. I don't mind at all." His gray eyes soften as he bows slightly and turns away.

I step into the barn, and I notice some fire lizards skittering over Pops's legs. There's one climbing up his arm, another sliding down his back—

"Pops!" I shriek, reaching for the nearest fire lizard. "Not again." They hiss and spit blue flames as I swat them away. I crunch my toe wherever their spittle lands.

Pops just blinks at me. Not even a question in his eyes. Just a dull, tired expression.

This is what happens when you veer into the wild parts of magic. You might not come back. You might not come home.

I read through Grandpa's diaries. Must have combed through them at least fifty times, searching for clues, some sort of cure. I found nothing.

But Pops was smart. He was a kind man, even to strangers. Strangers like Mr. Halifax who will spend long hours of the day searching for a cure. And now we have something to hold onto. All we have to do is show Pops a memory that will bring him back home.

Please, let this work.

I drag a crate next to Pops and take a seat, pinching Grandpa's journal between my fingers. I hear a fresh burst of chattering near the house. One of the speakers sounds like Daichi. Vida is laughing—or is that Mom? Yes, that's Mom. She's got a warble in her voice. She's laughing and crying.

"Vida just got home, Pops," I say. "With her husband."

"Hmmm," Pops says. This is the only thing he ever says.

I reach for his hand, but he yanks away.

"No, Pops. I need to take your hand, or it isn't going to work."

His eyebrows push down and his mouth slides open, but he says nothing.

"Please," I say, holding out my palm. He pushes my hand away again.

A sharp pain pinches my chest as I hold back the tears building behind my eyes.

Fuzzy Lips snorts and wiggles his lips, and this gives me an idea. I lean down and scoop a clump of hay into my palm.

"I'm going to read you a story, Pops." I flip Grandpa's journal to a page wrinkled with tear stains. This is where Pops poured out bittersweet memories right before he saved us all from a giant fire. "It's a beautiful story."

"Hmmm."

"It's full of heartache, but it has a happy ending. It reminds me of home."

Pops slows his breathing, blinks, and tilts his head.

Is that a nod?

I breathe in and read his journal entry out loud. And as I read, I study his eyes. I'm not sure. Are they glistening with tears? Or has he been staring at the sun for too long?

When I finish reading, I reach for his hand, palm open with a tuft of hay. Pops reaches for the hay and brushes my palm. A spark passes between our fingers, and the hay lights up like a match. Pops snatches the flame and stares as it glows in his fist, then seeps into his skin.

"Pops, are you in here?" Vida peers into the barn. Her hair is woven with those same purple flowers I gave to Chewbie. She smiles, her eyes glimmering, but there's a hint of sadness. Walking over, she carries something in the folds of her apron.

"Would you like one, Elby?" She digs into her apron and holds out her hand. Pinched between her fingers is a strawberry from our garden. Must be the last of the season. I pluck the strawberry—red, all the way to the top. I hold it to my nose and breathe. Smells like my childhood. Smells like Juniper.

"Wait a minute," I say and lean toward Pops, holding the strawberry under his nose.

"Hmm." He snatches the berry from my palm and breathes in its scent. When he pops the fruit into his mouth, his face pulls back in surprise.

"Pops? Are you okay? Are you with us?" I grip him by the shoulders, and this time he does not brush me away. Instead, a tear slips down his cheek.

His mustache curves and his glistening eyes spark orange.

Journal Entry

AUGUST 10, 1905

On their birthing day, Juniper came first. She wailed like a storm was coming out of her. It wasn't an angry scream. More like she wanted to tell everyone she was finally here.

Then came Finn. He was quiet. The calm after the storm. He was most at peace when he lay beside Juniper, which was fine because Juni would not sleep without him at her side. She'd scream like the devil whenever I moved her away from her brother. Sometimes, I'd wake to Juniper clutching Finn. Moira learned quickly that Finn must always be in Juniper's sight, or she'd cry.

She cried for both of them. When she was hungry, they were hungry. When she was hot, they were hot. When she soiled herself, she cried. When Finn soiled himself, she cried. She refused to eat before Finn took his first bite.

I knew early on she was destined to become a wild one like me. I saw it in the way her eyes took in the world. I saw the way she reached for the sun and gripped the earth in her hands like the wild belonged to her. And, of course, strawberries were her favorite food, especially since they also served as toys. She shook them like a rattle, tossed them like a ball, and squashed them like bugs.

I used to imagine what her future would be like. And later, after she passed, I used to torture myself with thoughts of what could have been. But I try not to think about that now. Those kinds of thoughts will turn a person mad. It's hard enough just remembering that night.

It started as a very long day. I left early to help a nearby village tame a building fire. It took all day to ride there, control the fire, then ride back home. I came home late into the night, exhausted. As soon as my head hit the pillow, I fell asleep.

Moira and I are still not sure how the fire started in our home, but I have my suspicions.

It could have been a neglected candle left burning overnight, or a stray spark from the wood-burning stove. Deep down, I can't help but wonder. Could it be me? Did I start the fire? The only times I lost control of my flame was when I first started using magic. I would have felt the magic slip out of my control. I would have known.

The truth is, I don't know what happened. And that kills me.

We do know this. At about three o'clock in the morning, Moira woke up to smoke and an orange glow coming from the hallway. She tried to shake me awake. At least, that's what she told me. She also told me to grab the babes, still sleeping in our room at the time. Then she left for the rest of the children.

But I kept sleeping.

This will be my biggest regret. Falling asleep again. I was so exhausted. I don't even remember waking up the first time.

Finally, the pop of fire reaches my ears, and I opened my eyes to a wall of orange flames climbing up the ceiling. I jumped from the bed, disoriented. For a second, I thought Moira had gotten lost in the fire, then I realized she was gone. She'd already run, so I turned for the babes.

I grabbed Finn and Juni and pushed my way through the flames. I demanded one last burst of magic from myself. That's when I felt something grow out the back of my shoulder blades—wings of fire. I'd never grown these before, maybe because I never needed them. I definitely needed them in that moment. I circled my wings around my babes as I crashed through the pillars of fire engulfing the hallway. I used my wings to break through the door and cover our heads as the house crumbled and sagged.

When I landed on the cold grass, I was sick with exhaustion. Almost fainted right there on the spot. But I was too scared to lose my wits. My babes needed to breathe. Finn took the first breath, just as Juniper would have wanted. But she didn't follow her brother. She didn't come back to us. She never breathed again.

I don't understand it. I never will. It weighs me down even now that my little wild one couldn't stay with us. But sometimes I wonder. Maybe she knew all along. It's like she was his guardian angel from the very beginning. And even now, it's like she's still watching over him while Finn plays with her in his imagination.

Finn inspires me. Because of his devotion to the memory of his sister, I also wanted to honor my daughter's memory. So, I planted strawberries in the garden a few months ago. It's the first time I tried growing them since Juni's death. I'm not sure why, but I haven't gone near the garden to make sure the clippings took to the soil. Maybe it was a mistake to plant them in the first place. Or maybe I'm just a coward.

Coward. This is the word that echoes in my mind every day. I once fought back flames and rescued villages, but now I've locked this magic away. I see Elbert's disgust with his natural-born magic. That disgust is with me, too. And for so many years, I stopped doing what I promised to do: protect my family. Instead, I hid from the flames, like a coward.

But now I will follow Juniper's example. I will protect Finn. I will protect all of them because they are all I have.

They are my home.

Acknowledgments

I'd like to start with Pops—my dad—Douglas "El Guapo" Tawlks (born a Padilla). Originally, Elbert was destined to leave his farm like so many origin stories, but something made me pause. The character Pops was too special for Elbert to leave behind. Pops was special because he reminded me of my dad in some ways. Thank you Dad for climbing out of your grief and shaking off your self-doubt. I've watched you turn the dark period of your life into a powerful testimony. You taught me to hope in spite of my failures. Don't forget to write your story down someday.

I can't thank my dad without next thanking my mom, Shari Tawlks. Thank you for being there at the very beginning, writing down my stories before I knew how to read, let alone pen letters.

I'd like to thank my Grandma, Lena (maiden name Dowden), for telling me all about apple orchard farming and clicking like, sharing, and commenting on all my author posts on Facebook.

Big thanks goes to the early, early readers: Stephanie Krier, Lyndsay Wilkin, Ashlie Guillot, Paul Gilberry, and the Peterson/Carpinelli kids!

Special shoutout to Hannah Muldery for going the long haul with me and reading my manuscript way more times than I should have asked. Words can't express how important your support is to me, and I can't wait to be your cheerleader when it's your turn to share your story.

Another shoutout goes to Teddi Deppner and the Havok

horde for pushing me to grow as a writer and taking me into the fold. #havok4life

Thank you to the rest of my family and friends for your support. Don't worry, Nicole. If I make it onto a talk show, you'll be my plus one.

Thank you to the Monster Ivy team! So much effort went into this project. I especially want to thank Amy Michelle Carpenter for seeing the heart of my story and taking me on. Thank you to the team for pushing me to reach a bit deeper and see how far this story can go.

A huge adoring thanks goes to my husband for being the first one I pester to re-read passages that have barely changed. I love you. I will always remember your confident words: "when you get published." Looks like you were right about this one.

Finally, I have to say thank you to my best friend, the one who saved my life, Jesus Christ. Thanks for being the reason grace exists.

Thank you all. I hope you find meaning in this story.

Krysta

About the Author

Krysta Tawlks is the author of Children of the Wild and several short stories. She grew up watching hot air balloons float by her small country house, spent a few years post grad in Thailand, humbling her Western mind, and currently teaches English skills to language learners. She lives with her husband and son in Northern California.

Printed in the USA
CPSIA information can be obtained
at www.ICGtesting.com
JSHW012202171023
50357JS00012B/38